THREE DREAMS DEEP

By D. F. Lamont

For Cecilia and my kids.

THREE DREAMS DEEP

CONTENTS

CHAPTER 1
TOPSY TURVY

"WILLIS. WILLIS? MR. NEWMAN? Are you awake? Or are you dreaming again?"

There was a whack of a yardstick on a desk, and Willis found himself startled awake, though not fully alert.

His head was spinning. Where was he? In class, obviously, but which one? Everything was very fuzzy. History? It felt like he hadn't attended all year. He quickly checked the corner of his mouth to see if he had been drooling. Dry! Phew.

Boy, am I out of it, he thought, and looked around to get a handle on where he was. The calendar says Friday. It's 2:35 pm, the last class of the day. There is a drawing of the solar system on the blackboard. And everyone is staring at me.

"I'm sorry Mrs. Vanderbilt. I just lost track."

"I know it's been a long week Willis, but let's pay attention," Mrs. Vanderbilt said. "As I was asking, how do we know the earth is round and not flat?"

Everyone's attention turned back to the front of the class and Willis sighed. Vernon had his hand up first, as he always he did. He was always also wrong.

"Oh! Oh! Mrs. Vanderbilt"

Mrs. Vanderbilt waited a minute, avoiding eye contact with Vernon, perhaps waiting for someone else to volunteer an answer.

"Oh! Oh! Pleease!"

"Yes, Vernon?"

"We have pictures from space!"

"Yes," she answered patiently, "But what

about before we went into space? How do we know the world is round, when our senses tell us it's flat, and that earth goes around the sun? It doesn't feel like we're moving, does it?"

Vernon deflated and drooped forward.

"As you sit at your desks, facing south," she continued, "you are going about 800 miles an hour sideways, as the earth spins on its axis. And the earth itself is flying through space around the sun at 66,000 miles per hour.

"That's not what our senses tell us - our eyes and ears, our balance. What feels more solid than the ground beneath our feet? It feels like we are standing still, and the sun goes around us. Are our senses lying to us?

"What Galileo and Copernicus did was imagine to the world worked in a way that their senses told them it didn't. They asked, "Are my senses deceiving me? Is there something more that what I can just feel, or see, or hear? Or if I use my imagination, and imagine a different world, maybe I can see that this new world is true, not just what I think I'm seeing. Because science isn't just about thinking – it's also about imagining and believing."

She looked at the class. There was silence. Vernon was staring back with a glassy look of incomprehension. Willis looked thoughtful, but he was really just putting it on for the benefit of Mrs. Vanderbilt.

The buzzer rang, blurring into a chaotic scraping of chairs, shuffling feet and chaos. Over the noise, she shouted out, "Have a good weekend and don't forget your term assignments are due on Monday!"

Monday? Where had the time gone? He hadn't done anything. He hadn't even been to the library. What was his topic again? Gravity. Gravity? Why, how had he picked that one?

∽

Willis was at the dinner table stabbing at his dinner with a fork and complaining to his dad, who was hunched over the sink, with a safety-pinned tea towel for an apron.

"What's the point of studying the crazy things people used to think about the way the world was? Like gravity, how obvious is gravity?"

"Well, Willis," his dad said, pushing his thick-rimmed glasses up his nose, "remember the time I wrote that piece on the initiation rites of the Xintuqhosa tribe in South America?" Here his dad made a series of clicking and popping noises, finishing with the sound of a bubble bursting three times.

"No."

"I used to read it to you as I was working on it. Would put you right to sleep. Short story long, I had a hard time understanding what they were doing, until I looked at it from their point of view. Sometimes the ideas we use are like the water for fish: they're so much part of the way we get around that we don't even know they're there until they're gone. Until you're flopping around on the dock, gasping."

His dad did a weird fishy dance with his hands flipping around at waist level.

"With gravity, people knew the world was round. They just couldn't figure out how someone on the other side of the world could stay on without falling off. They thought the world was like the one on the Sherwin Williams paint can, and ships would fall of the edge like you would slip off the edge of a domed roof."

"Here, look," he disappeared briefly and came back carrying a thick book with tissue-thin pages. "What does that say?"

"Antipodes. How do you say it - anty-poads?"

"It's ant-tip-o-dees. So imagine someone standing on the other side of the world from you right now. To you, their head is pointing straight down - into space, and their feet are pointing at you. So hundreds of years ago, when people thought of antipodeans, they thought of people whose heads were "below" their chests, but they would draw someone like this."

"That's weird," said Willis.

"It's just another way of looking at it," his dad said.

"A weird way of looking at it."

His dad turned and looked at the image.

"Hm. Yeah. I guess that is pretty weird. But no less valid!" he poked his finger in the air and shouted at the ceiling with a crazy grin. He always did that when conceding a point.

"What's the point in learning about gravity?" said Willis. "It's obvious that it's there, it's always been there, it'll always be there."

His dad leaned back and thought for a second.

"That's true – but even if gravity is always there, there was a time before we had a name for it. And there's more to learning than just repeating what's in a book. You have to absorb it, let it sink in. It's one thing to think about things, and it's another thing to believe in them in your bones."

"I guess," said Willis.

"You better get going if you're going to get to the library before it closes."

∽

The sun had set by the time Willis got downtown and reached the old public library. The air was damp & chilly and gusts of wind kicked up dead leaves across the stone steps. He could see the low clouds being driven across the sky, bluish grey behind the black facade of the library, silhouetted against the sky. It looked like an ancient Greek temple, squat with massive columns. In the short, wide triangle under the roof, blank-eyed statues huddled, staring out across the city.

He reached the entrance and almost crashed into Vernon, who was struggling under the weight of a duffel bag filled with sharp corners.

"A little light reading for the weekend?" Willis said. Vernon laughed nervously and staggered down the steps towards a waiting car.

Willis slipped inside and found that the old library seemed particularly dark and unwelcoming. By day the sunlight streaming through the tall windows into the wood-panelled interior seemed cosy, warm and welcoming.

Now at night he could see that many of the bulbs had burned out. The stacks of books were lit by yellow pools of light, like streetlights.

"Where would I find astronomy?" asked Willis.

Mrs. Finch the librarian, an older lady with a frizz of grey hair in a bun, sized him up over her reading glasses.

"Astronomy? Come with me."

They worked their way through a maze of shelves, each row empty of people. It seems much bigger than I remember, thought Willis. Or maybe it just seems that way at night. The shelves seemed to vanish in the distance.

Finally they reached a row of shelves up against the wall, where there was a sliding ladder to reach the uppermost levels of the bookcase.

Shelf after shelf was empty of everything but a faded outline of books that had sat unmoved for years, now gone.

"We've been nearly cleaned out, I'm afraid,"

This is a nightmare, thought Willis. "Is there anything left at all?"

"You're welcome to look, of course," said Mrs. Finch. There was the muffled sound of a desk bell tapped once, twice, three times impatiently.

"I'll have to get that. Take your time." She shuffled off.

Willis stared up at the shelves. Was that something there?

High, high up, in the deep shadow next to the light that was shining into his eyes. A tiny glint of gold on a bookbinding.

With a scrape and a squeal of brass wheels he pulled the ladder towards him and started to climb past the empty shelves. There, tucked into a corner and hidden in shadow, was a book. Its leather binding was dry, cracked and faded on the spine. The covers, which had been hidden from light, were a richer colour but still caked with dust.

He puffed to blow some of the dust free, sending thousands of glowing motes dancing in the beam of light nearby, but the title was still obscured. He rubbed at the embossed letters, revealing the words:

AFTRONOMIE ALCHEMIE AND THE KNOWNE UNIVERFE

There was an illegible signature underneath. He flipped through the book, past densely handwritten pages, strange graphs and calculations and royal blue charts of the night sky filled with constellations and monsters.

When he reached a map of the world he stopped. At regular intervals around the map it read "Edge of the Worlde" with drawings of sea serpents, whales, mermaids and mermen romping in the oceans.

I guess this'll have to do. Maybe I can use it for a kind of Show and Tell, he thought.

∽

Once home, Willis pored over the pages of the book, engrossed. It was full of riddles, puzzles and hints, mysterious drawings, mazes & monsters. There were whole worlds sketched out, Escher-style impossible buildings with looping staircases to nowhere, optical illusions where you stared at a pattern and suddenly something new and different would appear.

His dad leaned into his room against the door jamb.

"Lights out, Willis. It's late. Don't wear yourself out."

"I just want to get to the end of this page."

"All right. Then lights out for sure. Remember, I've got some meetings out of town tomorrow morning so you'll have the house to yourself for a few hours."

His dad closed the door softly.

Willis lay on his back with his legs up against the wall. Lying like this it was easy to imagine the world upside down, that if he stretched upwards and stood on his head, that he could walk around on the ceiling, clambering up the underside of the staircase.

Willis closed the musty-smelling book, sending up a cloud of dust, turned off his light, and went to sleep.

✍

It wasn't the bright daylight that streamed through Willis' windows the next morning that woke him up, but his discomfort.

Overnight his bed seemed to have become stiff as a board, and no amount of tossing or turning let him drift back to sleep.

He blinked himself awake. He wasn't in bed. He was lying on a perfectly flat, white smooth surface. Not the floor. He seemed to be at the bottom of a big white box.

He pushed his covers aside and looked around, and up, and froze. He was staring up at his own floor. Directly above him was his bed, the carpet, desk with papers pencils and pens apparently glued to the surface. They all loomed above him, ready to fall on his head at any minute.

His comforter and pillow were next to him on the ceiling. He jumped to his feet and peered out his doorway down the hallway.

All the furniture in the house was still stuck to the floor. The only things on the ceiling were himself, his bedclothes, and a chandelier in the hallway - which, from his point of view, was sticking up straight like a newly planted tree.

Gravity has been reversed for him – and him alone.

Willis walked around the house on the ceiling, stepping over the top frames of doorways. The ceiling of the stairs sloped smoothly up to the first floor at an unclimbable 45-degree angle.

It was an older house, with high ceilings, so everything was out of reach. He looked around for a phone to call his dad, only to find the portable where he had left it the night before: on a low side table, well out of reach.

Maybe that bookcase can hold my weight, he thought. There's nothing holding it to the floor, but maybe I can scramble up and get the phone.

He tested his weight on it on the underside of the top shelf. It seemed alright, though he was still leery of the bookshelf tipping over and crushing him. He started to clear some space for his feet by picking out books. As he pulled them loose they dropped to his feet - not "up" to the floor.

He tested a couple of other books. They dropped too.

Forget the bookcase, he thought. I'll just make a pile of books and stand on that. That was tricky too. None were the same size, some were slippery. He had slipped twice when he saw something on the floor out of the corner of his eye.

Someone, not something. A girl about his own age, looking up at him. Willis jumped back, startled, and stumbled backwards over the books, falling onto the ceiling.

"Who are you?" he said.

"Don't you remember me?" the girl said. She looked sad and disappointed. "We used to be best friends. Though I guess it's been a long time."

"We did?"

"Yeah. It was a few years back. I'm Sala."

"Sala? Sala."

Willis stared at her. She looked awfully familiar. "How did you get in?"

"I knocked on the door, and no one answered. It wasn't locked, so I came up," she said. "Why are you still wearing your pajamas? How did you get up there?"

Willis looked down – he had forgotten he was still in his sleeping gear.

"I woke up like this, and I haven't been able to reach my clothes to change," Willis said.

Maybe I won't have to do my project on gravity after all, he thought. Maybe I can just get my dad to take me to school. He had an image in his head of his dad struggling down the sidewalk, pulling him along bobbing and spinning like a helium balloon in the air.

It gave Willis an idea.

"Sala, in the kitchen closet there's a heavy-duty extension cord - can you get it for me?"

"Sure," Sala shrugged, and started down the stairs.

"Wait! Can you get me something to eat too?"

"Sure thing," she called back.

A few moments later she was back, carrying a bright orange cord and a couple of apples, which she tossed up to Willis.

"OK," said Willis, "See if you can pull me down to the floor."

In a second they were in a floor-to-ceiling tug of war. For a second there was no movement, then as Sala put all of her weight on the cord, Willis's feet lifted off the ceiling. Sala was almost being lifted off her feet.

"It's working!" said Willis, and he reached up - or down - to grab Sala' hand, just as she jumped up to grab his. They hung there for a moment, suspended in midair in a kind of equilibrium, each a few inches off the floor.

They both burst out laughing in amazement, then something tipped the scales. Sala's feet start to lift further off of the floor - higher and higher.

"Oh, no!" Sala said, and a moment later she crashed to the ceiling next to Willis.

"Are you OK?"

Sala nodded, and started to get up.

"Wait, take your shoes off so you don't get the ceiling all scuffed up," said Willis. Willis then helped Sala to her feet.

There they stood staring up at the floor, Willis in pajamas, Sala in stocking feet, with a pile of books scattered around them.

"I guess I should have asked you to give me the phone first," said Willis.

"Is it just us, do you think?" asked Willis. "If we can make it downstairs - or upstairs, or whatever, to the main floor - could we get help somehow?"

"I don't know," said Sala.

"How can we find out?"

"Why don't we drop something out the window?" she said.

"Hey - good idea!" said Willis, and he started looking around for something they could drop. Books, pillows and sheets all seemed like a bad idea. He grabbed one of the apples Sala had given him.

The living room windows were all shut, but the one in Willis' bedroom was open. He dragged it open a little more so they could both stick their heads out, put his arm out as far as he could and let go of the apple.

It fell away upwards into the sky, drifting a little sideways as a crosswind picked it up, then faded into infinity.

The two sat quiet for a moment.

"Well, that answers that question," said Sala.

"Does it?" asked Willis "Does it mean we'll never be able be able to go outside again or we'll fall into the sky?"

Sala didn't say anything.

The idea sank in. Willis slammed the window and together they took a frightened step backwards.

"Maybe if we just wait this out till my dad gets home, it won't get any worse."

There was a dry ticking sound, like the rattle of crisp leaves, or a patter of rain.

Small light objects were landing at their feet. A sprinkling of paper clips and a smattering of pencils, then a pair of nail clippers and a box of mismatched nuts, bolts, and screws that Willis usually kept on his desk, and now wished he had left in the basement workshop.

They glanced up and could see things falling up from the furniture - small objects were first, but larger objects - books and furniture - were starting to tip up at the edges. Willis glanced into the hallway, where the chandelier, which had stood up ramrod straight, was starting to wilt and tip over.

They were standing in a growing hail of objects – clothes, shoes, books, toys, dirty laundry, socks, pictures. A desk chair crashed down next to them, narrowly missing Willis' head.

Then there was the low a sickening groan followed by a deep cracking sound, like a tree trunk being split. The whole house shook, showering them with dust.

"What is happening?"

"I think your house is going to fall off the bottom of planet," said Sala.

The bottom of the planet? Willis' mind raced.

"I know - wait - that's what I was reading in that book!"

"What book?"

"The one I took out of the library for my project," said Willis. "Help me look for it."

He started to sift through the growing pile of objects at his feet, books and shoes bouncing off his head and back.

"It's not here - we'll have to look up on the floor."

There was another mighty snapping sound and the house shuddered again. Willis looked up.

"It's still there - on my bedside table. Get on my shoulders."

Sala climbed onto Willis' back and they swayed back and forth, before getting close to the desk. Sala stretched up to the book as the light and the alarm clock dropped past her face.

"C'mon - just a bit further - jump!" she grunted at Willis.

"You jump!"

"I've got it! - No!" she fumbled it and they fell sideways to the ceiling together as the desk crashed down next to them. The book skidded across the ceiling, but Sala snatched it back just before a computer monitor landed on top of it.

"Gimme," said Willis, and flipped through the pages. "Here. According to this map, we're at the bottom of the world."

"So?"

"I was thinking about this stuff before I went to sleep. We know now there is no bottom of the world – not since an apple fell on Newton's head and he realized how gravity holds everything together. It's all a matter of perspective."

There was a break in the rain of objects. Instead, the objects around their feet started stirring and lifting upwards.

Something in Willis' stomach did a somersault. The whole world flipped over like an hourglass, and Willis hit the floor of his bedroom with a thud, his desk, lamp and alarm clock crashing down next to him along with his desk chair.

He looked around. There was no Sala. No book. Everything was back perfectly in place, although the chandelier in the hallway was swinging slightly.

"What was that noise?" he heard his dad's voice from the other room.

His head was still spinning. What had just happened?

"I - I guess I just fell out of bed," said Willis.

"Are you all right?"

"Yeah, I'm fine. I just - I guess I'm just not awake yet."

"Well, my meeting was cancelled, so I'll make you some pancakes," said his dad. "I'll tell you, something funny just happened to me too. I was almost brained with an apple out of the clear blue sky!"

With that, his dad tossed him a granny smith apple - with a fresh bruise on the side.

CHAPTER 2
DREAM A LITTLE DREAM

WILLIS HAD NEVER taken a class in the history of science.

There was no Mrs. Vanderbilt.

There had been no assignment on gravity.

There was no exotic, ancient book, and no spooky downtown library.

Willis hadn't woken up on the ceiling.

His house hadn't almost fallen off the planet.

That was the weirdest dream I've ever had, Willis thought.

Or - no. Maybe he had had weirder dreams, but none so vivid, so real. In fact, the dream had seemed just as real - maybe more so - than what he was living right now.

He sat at the breakfast table in the clear, dull, grey light of day. There was a pancake in front of him and the smell of almost-burning butter in the air, along with brewing coffee, and the sharp note of fresh squeezed lemon. He and his parents would have lemon and sugar on their pancakes sometimes, instead of what his dad called "boring old syrup."

Was this breakfast real? Was he dreaming now? He looked over at his dad, who sat with his coffee mug clutched to his chest, reading the paper. He looked at his mom, who was pouring more batter into the pan. Are dreams ever this boring? Willis asked himself. Maybe that's how I know what's real and what isn't.

He looked at his own plate, sprinkled sugar over the pancake and squeezed a wedge of fresh lemon over it, carefully making sure every granule got a bit of lemon juice. He savoured the smell as it wafted up, cut out a piece of the pancake, folded it double onto his fork and put it in his mouth.

He closed his eyes and concentrated on the intense flavour, chewing slowly and deliberately. He never ate anything in dreams, nothing that tasted any good, and this was delicious. This must be real. He cut another piece, and chewed it the same way, then a third. He was lifting up a fourth forkful when he heard a snort.

"Good pancake, Willis?" said his dad.

He looked up. His dad's expression was blank but his mom was covering her mouth and trying not to laugh.

So he explained his dream, as his parents listened and laughed. The last minute term assignment he didn't know about in the class he didn't take from a teacher he didn't have; the magical book from a library that didn't exist; waking up on the ceiling of his room and getting a visit from Sala, who said she used to be his best friend.

"Wait a minute Willis, that last bit is true," said his Mom. "You did have a best friend named Sala. Don't you remember her?"

"No. I have no idea what you are talking about."

His mother pulled up to the table and sat with a coffee cradled in her hands while his dad cleaned up the dishes.

"When you were three and four years old," she said, "you had an imaginary friend named Sala. She travelled everywhere with you. She lived in a tree outside our house and she even came with us on vacation. You insisted, every night, that we had to set a space at the table for her. Sometimes I even had to put out food for her. When it was cold or rainy you made me go outside to check on her."

"Oh, did you two get into trouble," said his dad from the sink.

"When you misbehaved in front of guests," continued his mother, "or used some word you didn't pick up from me, we would say 'Where did you learn that?' and you would always say, 'It was Sala.' Poor Sala. She got blamed for a lot of things."

"What happened to her?" asked Willis.

"One day I was setting place out for her at dinner and you told me not to bother, because she had gone away and wasn't coming back. That was the end of her."

"She seemed so real."

"You certainly insisted that she was."

"No, last night," said Willis. "I felt like I remembered her."

"That's how dreams are sometimes. They stick with you."

Willis reached for the bowl of fruit that was sitting in the middle of the table and picked out a granny smith, turning it over thoughtfully.

⁊

Normally, Willis stayed up far later than his parents. But his dreams the night before left him feeling like he hadn't slept at all. His eyes were drifting closed as he sat on the couch in front of the TV with his parents.

"Enough already, go to bed!" his father had insisted, complaining that Willis' light snoring (and occasional nose whistling) was ruining his enjoyment of a rerun of a British comedy. Willis heaved himself towards the staircase.

"Willis, don't forget - you said you would drop off a meal for Margaret tomorrow. Your mom and I can't make it so you'll have to go."

Oh no. At the reminder, his feet grew ankle weights and the steps in front of him stretched and extended away from him like the ladder on a fire truck.

Mad Meg. He would have to go over to her creepy house, with its peeling paint and rooms that had sat untouched for years. He might even have to talk with her.

"Willis, please don't just drop it off like you're delivering a pizza. Visit with her for a little while. You know how much she likes your company."

Enjoy? Mad Meg didn't seem to enjoy much

of anything, though she did moan and carry on when Willis left.

Once in bed, Willis' eyelids felt heavy, his body drained of energy, but he still felt a flicker of unease about drifting off. He was on the verge of sleep when he had the sensation that someone tipped him out of bed on a board. He clutched at the mattress, head spinning. He rolled over, settling himself tight in his comforter. When he finally settled it was into a dreamless sleep.

∽

Willis stopped at the foot of Mad Meg's sidewalk. The air was cold and damp, and through the bottom of the cardboard box he was carrying he could feel warmth radiating from the foil-wrapped containers and plates. A roasted chicken leg, buttery mashed potatoes, carrots, peas, even a slice of pie.

He looked up the sidewalk, like a crooked grey diving board over a green-black lake. On the right side of the two-story house there was a loose rain gutter, shot through with rust, swinging with each gust of wind. The massive brick chimney looked like a ruined castle. Paint was peeling off the grey clapboard siding in long, loose curls like strips of paper.

Willis looked from window to window. One had been long ago been patched over with a sheet of plywood, its pale golden tones now weathered to a cracked grey. Other windows were filled in just with cardboard and tape.

He glanced up to the second floor and was startled to see the darkened silhouette of Mad Meg's head and shoulders. She was standing perfectly still and staring straight out of the window.

Willis jumped a little, and let out a tiny scream that sounded like "Yip!" and instantly felt embarrassed.

A man just walking past with his little dog gave Willis a dirty look. The little poodley thing had scampered away in terror when Willis jumped.

"Sorry," he said, but the man was being

dragged off and didn't hear.

Now he felt ridiculous. Just get it over with, he thought.

Balancing the box in the crook of his arm, he knocked twice on the heavy front door, then let himself in. In the front hall, the walls were a dirty syrupy-yellow and the living room looked like something from a museum. Old furniture, old-fashioned phone, all topped with fine grey dust.

"Hello?" His voice was loud in the quiet house.

"Who is that?" it was Meg's voice, very worried.

"It's just Willis, Mrs. Madden," he shouted up the staircase. "I've got your dinner."

"Oh. Come up, then."

He found her sitting in her usual spot, on a couch in a den. She was wearing pajamas and an old housecoat, her face worn and lined with sorrow. She had dark smudges under her eyes and her hair was smushed to one side, where she had been sleeping. She had a very old TV

34

running, not tuned to any channel in particular. The image was half snowy noise with a wiggling grey stripe that kept rolling upwards. She kept staring at it.

"Hi Mrs. Madden - I've got some food for you."

She looked up at him and brightened for a moment.

"Is that really you?"

"Yes, it's me. Willis Newman. You remember my parents? They're old friends of yours and asked me to bring over dinner."

Her eyes darted back and forth as she searched for something familiar in Willis' face. She looked lost and confused, and terribly sad, her mouth pulled down hard at the corners. Then her face relaxed.

"Of course. Willis. I remember you now. Sit down, sit down."

Willis unpacked the food onto a tray for her. It was always hard for him to believe that his parents had ever been friends with Mad

Meg, or that they were anywhere close in age. He remembered a family picture of her with his mum and dad, looking so young he could barely recognize any of them. Now his parents looked old, but Meg seemed ancient.

She ate a couple of forkfuls of mashed potatoes, but soon put her knife and fork together and pushed the plate aside.

"I'm not feeling very hungry just now. I'll finish later."

She lay down on the couch, and stared up at the ceiling. Then she winced as if she were in terrible pain, and a tear rolled down her cheek. She looked over to the TV screen. Willis had no idea what to say. This was the worst he had ever seen her.

"Are you okay, Mrs. Madden?"

Instead of answering, she covered her eyes with her arm, like she was trying to shield her face from a blow, or hide her face in shame, and sobbed.

"It's coming down," she said. "It's coming

down. The sky's all black and I just, I just can't see where the light is going to come through." Her body trembled, hard, as she gasped and tried to hold in another sob.

"Do you need me to get someone - I can call my parents," Willis reached for the phone, an odd pinkish-grey colour with a rotary dial.

"No, no," Mad Meg composed herself quickly. "I'm sorry I get like this. But my body aches and no matter how much I sleep it never seems to be enough, and I get so emotional. Could you pass me some of those?" She gestured for some tissues, and Willis passed her the box.

She blew her nose noisily and seemed to recover somewhat.

"You should go. Thank your parents for me. They've always been good friends, very good friends to me."

Willis stood up to go. He gestured toward the TV.

"Can I at least fix your TV for you? You've got such lousy reception I could probably…"

"NO!" she said, sitting up, with a fierce look on her face. Then she relaxed back again. "No. The fuzz helps - it makes the people more familiar. Sometimes I think I see people I know, old friends, and if it's too clear I realize it's not them."

Willis was taken aback. She had never acted like this. Then her eyes focused on him, and she seemed to sense his discomfort. She smiled a wry, crooked half-smile.

"I know that's crazy. Put it this way: it's still better than most of what's on TV."

Willis had to laugh. He could finally see why his parents would be friends with her.

She leaned back and pulled a blanket over herself.

"If you can lock the front door behind you on the way out I'd appreciate it."

The door of the den closed with a click. Normally he would be greeted with the staircase, a bathroom door and three closed doors to mystery rooms. Tonight the door of the room next to bathroom was ajar.

He peeked in. Perfectly ordinary. Like the living room downstairs, it was a moment frozen in time from ten years ago - this time of a boy's bedroom, unnaturally neat. He could see old comics, with yellowing pages and missing covers, on a shelf in a perfectly square pile, next to some old-looking toys staring sadly in the gloom.

He heard a shift and a groan, and the creaking of old furniture as Mad Meg tried to get comfortable on the coach. She coughed and blew her nose again.

His expedition over, Willis hurried down the stairs, pulled the self-locking front door tight, till the latch made that satisfying 'click.'

Outside on the porch, he took a deep breath. Only now that he was outside did he realize how nervous he'd felt.

He jogged down the walk, eager to distance himself from the house. He had the irrational feeling that he felt would be home free once he got to neutral ground of the sidewalk, but even then he wanted to speed away from her property. He slowed his pace to a fast walk once he got past her fence.

The first stars were starting to come out, and he could see Venus shining brightly beside the moon. The clouds had cleared off and the effect was like taking a blanket off the landscape. The day's warmth was gone. Willis fumbled to zip his jacket up to his chin and stuffed his hands into his pockets to keep them warm.

Poor Meg. She had really taken a turn. His parents should know. But it would be hard to explain.

He glanced back at her house. There, framed by a yellow rectangle was Mad Meg standing and staring out the window, at something far away.

A gust of wind kicked up some dead leaves and drove an icy chill across Willis' neck. Covering his face with the collar of his jacket, he quickened his pace and hurried home.

⁓

The next morning at breakfast he talked with

his Mom and Dad about his visit with Meg. He wasn't able to explain it much more than to say she had really creeped him out.

His mother had looked at him very seriously across the breakfast table over the top of her glasses.

"Mrs. Madden is not 'creepy,' Willis," she had said. "She is depressed, and you should be more understanding."

"What's she got to be so depressed about?" Willis asked. His mother glared at him and said nothing, while his father shook his head in disappointment.

"That's not always how it works, Willis," said his mother. "Maybe you're too young to fully understand."

On the weekend Willis passed Meg's house again, as he was walking home on a grey Saturday afternoon. It was mid-October, and the trees were reaching sadly into the sky with their long ash-grey fingers. The grass was brown and dry and it looked wintry. For all that, it was still surprisingly warm.

In the daylight, without lights to show any sign of life, her house looked grim and abandoned.

He stopped for a moment to stare, then caught sight of her standing at the same window, holding a curtain to one side and staring into the distance. He waved at her but she didn't seem to see him, but just kept staring.

Halfway down the block he walked past the squat three-story apartment building where he had lived with his parents when he was small. Next door there was a big grassy lot where an old house had been torn down and nothing had ever been rebuilt, fringed with big trees.

That's where I was friends with Sala, he thought to himself. And there's the old treehouse where I used to play with the neighbourhood kids before we moved to our new house.

He checked the time. He was early. Lots of time to get home. The shack was in a massive cottonwood, with huge trunk and massive branches that stuck straight out. There had been boards nailed into a ladder up the trunk, but a couple were missing and a few of the ones that remained sagged under his weight. He gave them a yank to test them. They seemed sturdy enough. He climbed carefully skyward.

He had his arms and shoulders over the lip of the door and was ready for the final push when the rusted-out nails on the board he was standing on gave way.

His legs were kicking and scraping in midair, a dozen feet above hard packed earth that would be no fun to fall onto. He managed to pull himself up, like he was getting out of the edge of a pool, squirmed over the edge and dropped to his back on the floor.

He lay there panting, staring up at the boards. Between the thin white strips of light from outside, the slats were covered with inky scrawls and blasts of spray paint, burn marks from lighters and matches. Then names upon names, carved all over the ceiling and walls. Some big, some small, some right across and through each other. Lots of names in hearts and "4-EVERS".

He wondered if his name was still here. It had been a long time. He had used that penknife that his grandfather had given him. It had slipped and given him a nasty cut once, right in the web of skin between his thumb and forefinger, and it had taken a long time to heal. Yes, there it was - a thin white line. He massaged the spot absent-mindedly with the other hand.

He had tried to carve his name in the corner, away from where everyone else was carving theirs, in the hope that it might last. He shuffled over to the corner and looked. It took a while, but there, masked by the shiny black spray paint of someone's name, was carved the word

WILLIS

in pointy letters.

That was a long time ago, he thought. He'd had to sneak up here when the big kids weren't hogging it. He looked around to see if he could see the names of the kids they used to hide from, like Tony and Stan. Tony's was easy to find. It was in letters four inches high, written across the width of three boards. Stan's initials, S.H., showed up in a few hearts.

Willis' eyes wandered back to the corner near his own name when he froze. His eyes had drifted across a name, its signature as familiar to him as the word. In neat, small letters, almost like handwriting, was carved "SALA."

"Don't you remember coming up with me when we carved our names here?"

Willis spun around, and there she was: Sala. Sitting behind him cross-legged, smiling and fiddling with a pebble in one hand.

"No - I. Am I dreaming again?'

"Yeah. How are your mom and dad?"

"They're fine - they said you're my imaginary friend."

"So?" said Sala, "I still had dinner at your house every night for more than a year. We went on vacation together. Remember the long car trips in summer?"

Willis searched his memory. He recalled sitting in a roadside diner, the walls and booths a deep maroon colour, drinking a Coke as a treat from a little glass. The smell of French fries splashed with vinegar, his dad's favourite. Their booth was next to a plate glass window. The gravel parking lot next to the highway outside, was incandescent in the summer sun.

He closed his eyes for a moment to concentrate on recalling the image. His mother was there, and his father, talking to a waitress who was being patient with his picky order. Next to his plate were a knife, fork and spoon tightly wound in a paper napkin. Sitting next to him on the bench was a girl his age, blowing bubbles in her milk, hair the colour of dark chocolate, pulled back in two braided pigtails. She gave him a mischievous sideways look.

Sala.

"Don't you remember any of this?" said Sala.

"Little bits," said Willis. "I feel like we've met

and that I know you but..."

"Doesn't this feel real?" said Sala.

"Yes! That's what's confusing."

"Why is it confusing?"

"Well," said Willis. "You're not real. You're a figment of my imagination. Just one part of my brain talking to another part of my brain"

"I am real," said Sala. "A lot more real than you think. I am just a different kind of real."

"What's that supposed to mean?"

Sala paused. "I really was your best friend when we were little. I was there," he said. "We live in different levels of reality, you and me. How can I explain it? It's like you live on the land, and I live in the sea. When we were kids, we played on the beach, where those two worlds kind of run into each other."

"So you're a fish?" said Willis.

"I am not a fish," said Sala.

"A mermaid?"

"Don't be a jerk. But where I live is a different level - a different world with different rules. The further away you get from the other world - like going inland, or far out to sea - the less they affect each other. But there are places where they sort of touch against each other and when we were friends it blurred together."

"But this is still a dream," said Willis. "You have a dream, you wake up and you forget it."

"No. No," said Sala, and she was very serious. "It is more than that. What about the other night? Where I helped you keep your house from falling off the planet."

"That's a perfect example!" said Willis. "I would have woken up, freaked out, but fine."

"If you hadn't woken up - or I hadn't shown up to help you out - what would have happened?"

"Nothing!" Willis laughed.

Sala shook her head in a disappointed way, and poked her finger skyward. Willis had a brief image of himself tumbling upwards into a clear blue sky, like a skydiver plummeting without a parachute, in reverse. He frowned slightly.

"Are you telling me I would have fallen up

into the sky?"

"It wasn't an ordinary dream," said Sala. "You know that. You were already in one dream, then you went to bed and had another dream. You were two dreams deep. That's where you crossed the line. From your world - back into mine. you could have fallen out of that window and kept falling."

Willis had a vision of himself, clutching at an unopened parachute, soaring ever upwards, up through clouds, mist condensing cold and wet on his skin, his fingers growing stiff as he struggled in vain to pull a ripcord to slow his ascent. The earth, receding below him, was getting hazy blue as the sky above turned slowly bluer-black, the air a bitter cold. An icy-cold draft blowing across his neck through the treehouse boards made him shudder and brought him back into the moment.

"You - we - can move back and forth between your reality and the dream world. It's like a bridge - or a ladder," said Sala. "I used to be more in your world, when we were little."

"What happened?" said Willis.

"I don't really know," said Sala. She stammered, and sounded very sad and tired. "People grow up. Their dreams get smaller. They forget their old friends, and drift deeper into their own worlds."

Sala lowered her eyes. Willis thought it looked like she might cry.

"There's another level," said Sala, her voice cracking. "Three dreams deep - it's like an ocean of magma beneath everything. Not that it's hot, but it's this place where you start to lose everything that makes you your own person. Up here, we're all different and separate at other levels, but down there, it's like they're all melted and mixed together and lost."

Willis sat in silence, afraid to interrupt. A chill ran down his spine, but it wasn't the draft.

"My brother's there. Miles," Sala.

"Miles?" Willis whispered to himself. He felt a twinge of memory, like the fleeting shadow of a bird passing overhead. "Miles?"

"Do you remember him?"

"I... I don't. Maybe I do? There's something, but I can't bring it back."

"You don't remember this?" Sala pointed to a spot on the wall. Willis peered at it. Next to a long drip of glossy red spray paint there was a heart drawn in black permanent marker. In the middle it said "Willis + Sala" in round loopy printing.

Willis' cheeks burned red. "I don't remember ever writing that!"

It wasn't quite enough to make Sala laugh, but it did make her smile.

"I wrote it," said Sala. "I guess I had crush on you. The three of us played together all the time. I would have tea parties, which you didn't mind because I always had cupcakes."

A wave of dizziness passed over Willis. He felt the treehouse spin around him like a top, and he covered his eyes with one hand.

"I'm sorry," said Willis. "This whole imaginary life I've had. This just sounds like too much. It's hard to take it all in."

"It's NOT imaginary!" said Sala. "It was real for me, and real for Miles. We wouldn't be where we are if it were still real for you!"

"Me? I don't know what you are talking about."

"I don't know how it works. But when you and me stopped being friends, Miles and I were cut off from the world you live in."

Willis sat and stared at Sala, not knowing quite what to think. She looked hurt and disappointed. Willis felt bad for her.

"Why do you need my help?"

Sala shrugged again. "A bunch of reasons, I guess. You can still move between dream-worlds. I don't know anyone else. Because we're the only ones who will do it. And because we were friends."

A gust of wind shook the entire tree, and the boards of the treehouse creaked in protest.

Willis scanned the walls, looking over all the names scribbled there. Some were familiar, but he couldn't recall faces, or last names. Others brought back vivid snapshot memories: that kid from across the street offering him red licorice string from a crumpled brown paper bag; that time that bully Joey was picking on a smaller kid, got decked and all the kids cheered.

"So let's say I do it," said Willis. "How does it work?"

"When you're in a dream, try to remember to go to sleep."

"That's it?"

"If I'm around, I'll try to remind you."

"How do I get out? What if I get stuck?" he shook his head, uncertain again. "How do I know if any of this is real?"

"Look," said Sala, "what about the apple that dropped out of the sky onto your dad's head? That shows my world and yours can still bleed together, like - colours in a painting. And two dreams deep, you can get end up getting cut off from your world. But I can help get you back."

"How?"

"Here," said Sala. She reached into the

pocket of his jacket and pulled out a pocketknife and a bright green granny smith apple, flecked with spots. She carved a chunk off the apple and popped it into her own mouth, then held the rest out to Willis. Catching a whiff of its tangy aroma, Willis realized he was very hungry, and his mouth watered slightly. Sala folded up the pocketknife and slipped it back in her pocket.

"Are you ready to wake up?"

"I guess so."

Sala lunged forward and shoved Willis out of the treehouse. Her hands caught Willis square in the chest, knocking the wind out of him. Willis tumbled backwards toward the ground, twisting like a cat and landing with a crash in a tangled heap on his bedroom floor, his leg wrapped around the cord to his clock radio.

He righted himself. In his hand was the Granny Smith apple - with the side freshly sliced off.

Chapter 3
Air

WILLIS WAS AWAKE but hadn't opened his eyes. Yet. Sunlight passed across his face, illuminating his eyelids, and he could see a reddish-orange glow with a tangle of blurry, spider-webbed lines in it. Then the inside of his lids went dark again.

The side of his face was pressed uncomfortably against some textured plastic-y fabric, and he could hear three competing strains of noise: a deep roar, a mechanical whine and a high-

55

pitched irregular whistle.

His head lolled and he opened his eyes. He was on a plane, and it was banking, apparently turning right on a final approach to land. Through the window next to him the sky was cloudy with patches of blue and glimpses of sunlight. Through the windows across the aisle, he could see the ground at a wonky angle.

There was a highway and a cloverleaf junction, swarming with tiny cars, the landscape encrusted with blocky, putty-coloured concrete buildings sticking up, crisscrossed with electrical lines.

He blinked hard. How long had he been asleep? The cabin shook.

The captain's reassuring voice came over the intercom.

"Ladies and gentlemen - we're just experiencing a little clear air turbulence. We've got some delays at one of the airstrips but we should have you on the ground shortly."

He felt a clunk and heard the whine of

hydraulics as the landing gear descended.

What is going on? Willis thought. Aren't we ever going to get to the airport?

They seemed to be flying towards the centre of town, dropping steadily. Out his window, not far past the buildings there a lumpy and rounded mountain, thick with green trees.

The plane was now at the same level as the tops of apartment buildings and skyscrapers - and close. So close that Willis could see someone standing leaning against their balcony railing, staring back at him as the plane soared by.

They dropped further, now flying between buildings, only a few stories above the ground. Willis looked around to see how other passengers were reacting - the cabin was half empty. No one seemed to be bothered much. Just ahead and across the aisle a man in a suit was sitting doing the crossword with headphones on.

Through a window across the way, Willis could see the whole plane briefly reflected in the mirrored windows of an office tower, then they started to descend past a row of electrical towers carrying high-tension lines. The lines dipped and flowed rhythmically as the plane dropped lower and lower.

They dipped into a canyon of buildings, whose fronts flashed by the window in a blur, some scarily close. It looked to Willis as if the wingtips might hit a building at any moment.

Then they were out in a more open space, just above a highway. Pressing his face to the window and looking down, Willis could see cars screeching to a halt and pulling over, scattering under the roar of the jet engines. They were headed straight for a tall highway overpass, a solid grey concrete roadblock spanning the highway.

The plane then dropped so hard and fast that Willis' stomach did a somersault. The plane flew under the bridge and his body floated upwards, his seatbelt tightening, keeping him from smashing into the ceiling, then he was thrown forward as the plane touched down, hard. The whole aircraft lurched and skidded as the wheels slammed against the highway, then the engines were put into reverse.

They had landed on one half of a highway. There were no cars around them, but traffic going the other way had gridlocked as everyone stared at the plane. People were getting out of their cars and running over, kids were pointing. He saw a chain reaction of accidents as one driver, staring in amazement at the plane, rear-ended the car in front of them.

There was a click of static and the Captain's soothing drawl came over the intercom "Sorry about the unusual landing, folks. We've made arrangements and we should be getting you to the terminal shortly."

Willis realized he had been holding his breath - he wasn't sure how long for. He loosed his grip on the armrests and leaned back, taking a deep breath. He wiped the sweat from his forehead.

No one else on the flight seemed perturbed. The businessman across the aisle seemed to treat it as part of an inconvenient routine. He took off his headphones, shook his head in disappointment, and looked at his phone to check for messages.

They arrived at the Terminal - a huge box of black steel girders and glass, and walked through milling crowds of travellers. Willis felt like he was being carried along in a river of people, being tossed around by currents and countercurrents, flowing around people standing talking with their luggage, before finally emerging in a relatively more open space, where he saw his parents.

Each was staring in a different direction, with a dim, unfocused look on their face, like they were in a trance. A boring trance. It was the kind of look his dad would get at the grocery store when he was tired and couldn't find the right aisle for spaghetti. Standing there, mouths agape.

"Mom! Dad!" They both jerked awake and started looking around, in that slightly panicked way that made them look very silly and slightly vulnerable. They still didn't see him.

"Over here! Here!"

Willis pushed his way through the crowd,

buffetted by shoulders and suitcases on wheels. He was only a few feet away and his parents still hadn't spotted him.

"I'm so glad you're here!" Willis said.

They finally turned to him. His dad's glasses were covered with greasy fingerprints that made his eyes hard to see. His mother shifted uncomfortably and wouldn't look at him.

"Ah, Willis!" his dad bent at the waist and extended a hand to shake it. That's a little stuffy, thought Willis, who was expecting a hug. His father, too seemed to be looking at a fixed point over and behind him. Willis checked back over his shoulder to see if there someone else they might have recognized was approaching, but there was just a milling crowd.

"You wouldn't believe what just happened," said Willis. "I can't wait to get home."

His parents said nothing. They stood still, looking down and past each other.

"There's no easy way of saying this - we won't be going home. Or - you won't be coming home with us."

Willis stared.

"We want you to meet someone," his mother added. "Down this escalator."

She gestured toward a curved railing that sank to the floor behind her.

They stepped over to the escalator, which stretched down over two or three stories. Willis could see someone standing at the bottom - a woman's legs, anyway. He couldn't see her face or upper body - they were blocked by a sign hanging from the ceiling. He stepped onto the steel steps with his parents and put his hand on the thick rubber handrail, which seemed to skip and slide at a different speed than the stairs.

The woman came into sight. Willis thought she looked to be about his mom's age, although there was something very old-fashioned about the way she was dressed that made her seem older. She had glasses with heavy cats-eye frames, and hair piled into a glossy black beehive, and was wearing a matching short skirt and jacket, in a pastel green colour. She looked like someone's grandmother from an old picture.

"That," said his father, "is your real mother. She's taking you home with her."

It was Mad Meg.

Willis' heart sank. For the first time in his life, he realized what it meant for your blood to run cold. His hands and feet - especially his fingers and toes - were suddenly icy cold, almost tingling. He twisted around to talk to his parents, who were standing on the escalator step behind him.

"What are you talking about?"

"You were adopted, Willis," said his mother, "and Margaret - your real mother - wants you back. She'll take good care of you." Again, they didn't look at him. He strained to see his father's eyes, but his glasses were white squares, smudged with fingerprints and reflecting the grey-white panels of fluorescent lights.

He turned back. Mad Meg saw him now and her face lit up with recognition. Willis had never seen her like this - young and brimming with delight. She stretched her arms out to him and bounced on her feet with excitement, her smile showing some of her too-red lipstick, some smudged on her teeth. He heard someone calling his name - but not a woman's voice.

"Willis!"

He craned his neck around, and so did his parents, but as before they seemed befuddled.

"Willis!" came the shout again. It was Sala, and she was at the top of the up escalator. There was an edge to her voice. "Those aren't your parents! Jump over and come up!"

His parents - or at least the people who, until that moment, Willis had thought of as his parents, had caught sight of Sala and were staring at her. Mad Meg's expression changed horribly: in a moment she had aged decades, her open smile gone, her mouth pulled down at the corners in a twisted mask of grief.

Willis glanced across at the other escalator. Between him and escape, there was a slippery stainless steel gulley, eighteen inches wide. Willis leapt over the railing, his feet sliding on the polished metal, and grabbed hold of the black rubber handrail.

He threw himself over the second rail, his hip landing hard on the wide steel step.

His parents lunged for him, and his father/not-father managed to get a hold of his jacket. He shrugged out of it and started sprinting up the escalator steps, two and three at a time, carried swiftly upwards and away from them, as his father/not-father tripped at the bottom of the steps where the moving escalator met the unmoving floor.

Sala was there at the top of the steps, her eyes shining.

"C'mon," she said, "Follow me, quick"

Sala threaded her way through the crowd, half-jogging, half-running, ducking and weaving through gaps, slowing and checking to make sure Willis was close behind.

"Hey - you kids!" a security guard shouted and started to jog after them.

"Where are we going?" shouted Willis.

"Just follow me!" said Sala. She pushed through a crowd of people at a baggage carousel, waiting to pick up their luggage, and jumped onto the moving conveyor belt, leaping over bags as she ran towards a trapdoor in the stone wall through which the belt ran.

She crouched down and walked crabwise through the curtain of black rubber flaps that acted as a gate, and disappeared. Willis could hear the grinding of gears, the squeal of machinery and the thumping of heavy baggage. His mind pictured a room full of tightly intermeshed cogs and gears, like a meat grinder ready to nip off a finger or grind him to nothing.

He hesitated for a moment, though the belt kept pushing him inexorably towards the hatch. He would either have to jump off and backtrack through the crowd - losing Sala - or go through.

"You!" There was a security guard scrambling onto the belt to catch him.

Willis didn't have any more time. He ducked

his head, half-closed his eyes and pushed his way through the curtain. The conveyor belt dumped him, in an awkward somersault, onto the ground. The roar of machines disappeared so quickly he thought he had been deafened. He was blinded by a shattering white light directly above him.

CHAPTER 4
WATER

THE DAZZLING LIGHT was the noonday sun in a deep blue summer sky, with cotton-ball clouds dotting the horizon. Willis was standing at the edge of a grassy field. A gentle breeze was blowing. He could smell fresh-cut grass and hear the drone of a gas lawnmower not far off, choking on some particularly indigestible piece of turf.

He looked back at the square hole he had just come out of: a dog hole in a chain-link fence. There was a baseball diamond nearby, and the faded lines of a football field painted on the grass, which had gone brown in patches.

Sala was brushing some cuttings off her knees.

"What the hell just happened?" said Willis, panting. The sun was warm on his skin, but he had broken out in a cold sweat. His hands and feet still felt cold and his heart was pounding hard in his chest. It felt like he had swallowed a rock.

"Those weren't your parents, if you hadn't figured it out."

"Yeah," Willis said, trying to catch his breath and relax the knots of tension in his gut. "Who were they?"

Sala sat down on a worn wooden bench, split and bleached by the sun, and Willis sat down next to her, panting.

Sala rubbed her chin. "They're from the other level. Everyone kind of blends together down there. You could call it the 'collective unconscious' I guess. They work together to get people to join them. And that was their way of recruiting you."

"Recruiting me to do what?"

"To join them," said Sala. "To be part of it. They're not always that bad at it, but they can be kinda dopey."

"Dopey? They scared the crap out of me," said Willis.

"It's kind of hard to explain," said Sala. "But if they're all together, on their own turf, they can be tougher to deal with. When they're out of their element, pretending to be something they're not - your parents or whatever - they just aren't as sharp."

"How did we get here? Did you make that happen?"

Sala smiled and shook her head. "I just know a few short cuts."

"So - can we just do anything now that we're here in the dream?" said Willis. "Why don't we just fly like Superman?"

"I don't know," said Sala. "That's not the way it seems to work."

"But it's a dream - we can do anything!"

"Can you do anything you want in your regular dreams?"

Willis mulled over the question. The answer was obviously no. When he did have flying dreams, they were almost always lame. When he dreamt of flying, it tended to be at walking speed, with his head at the regular height above the ground, only with his body stretched out behind him, like he was lying face down, being pushed along on a very tall hospital gurney. Occasionally he would drift to a stop and have to put one of his legs down, kicking the ground to get himself going again.

In other flying dreams Willis remembered beating his arms madly to get aloft, only to get caught like a kite in a tree.

The sun was warm on Willis' neck. He could hear a fly buzzing on and off, tracing circles, landing, then zipping away again. He realized he was relaxing, and took a deep breath. Sala sat next to him, hunched over and shredding a long blade of grass.

"Where do we go now?"

"Come on," said Sala, standing up and stretching. "We can start over here."

She started walking across the sports field to the line of trees, and Willis got up to follow her.

"It's weird," Sala said as they walked across the field. "It's not like where you're from. There're mountains and rivers and lakes and deserts, but they don't all act the same like they do for you. Sometimes, instead of being like different parts of a country, it's like walking from one room to another, like we did just now. Sometimes there are shortcuts and secret passages. Some of them are only one way - like a turnstile or a revolving door. You can't go back."

They were approaching the trees, and Willis caught the scent of water, and heard the ripple and burble of water on rocks. The line of trees sheltered a riverbank, and as they got closer he could hear a building roar of noise. There was a wide river, flowing fast, its water dark and clear. It must have been almost a mile across, and the far side was dotted with trees over a rocky shoreline.

"Sometimes," Sala said, "there is no shortcut. And nowhere to go but forward. We need to get downstream."

"By boat?"

"We'll have to go on foot."

There was no defined path to follow in the tangle of brush and trees. The ground was irregular with deadfall, and they sometimes had force their way through, over and past rotten stumps, slippery moss and thickets. It was hot going, and once they were deeper into the forest, gusts of tiny biting bugs would swarm up and fly into their eyes and mouths. For the most part they travelled in silence, although Sala muttered "Sorry" when a thin branch she had pushed past whipped back and stung Willis on the cheek.

They had been slogging through the woods for a while, the forest getting wilder and rockier all the time. The quiet of the sports field soon seemed impossibly far back.

Willis paused and looked back to see if he could catch a glimpse of the open field they had left behind. There was nothing. The tangles of branches were closing together and knitting an impenetrable wall of greenery behind them.

Sala was up ahead on a ridge. She called down to Willis. "There's no going back, not from here."

The brush soon became impassable and they were driven to the shoreline of the river, the only place that was clear. There were no gentle muddy slopes here, as there had been near the field: instead there were rugged black boulders, some massive and sharp-edged, some rounded, wet and slippery-green.

The river had narrowed and was running faster. The going was very slow, and it was hard to get a steady footing. Again and again, Willis' feet slipped with a splash into the shallows, sometimes wedging his ankle painfully between stones.

Then they came to a corner. A rock twelve

feet high and shaped like a stone ax head jutted out over the water. The "blade" of the rock sloped inward to shore at the top and bottom, and stuck out the most in the middle. It looked supremely awkward to get around.

About eight feet out in the river there was a huge, smooth, standing wave, like blue-black glass.

Willis and Sala stood sizing it up, panting and feeling the cold water run around their ankles. Willis ducked down, trying to catch sight of the other side of the rock.

"Once we're past this, the going gets a bit easier," said Sala. "There are some rocky beaches on the other side."

Sala took an awkward step forward and tried several grips, trying to get a decent grip on the rock, but it offered no easy handholds. Willis could see that she was concentrating very hard. She took a couple of tentative steps, legs wide apart, then brought her feet awkwardly together on a small rock near where the rock jutted furthest into the river.

She swung her arm and leg quickly around and froze. She was splayed around the edge of the rock like a starfish, but her hold looked solid. For an instant she shot a cracked smile and an excited look of relief back at Willis. Then her right handhold failed.

She clawed desperately at the rock for a moment then tumbled back into the river and was swept away.

Willis lunged forward to catch her then stopped himself short, slipping and stumbling on the rocks. He peered out around under the ax-head rock, and saw Sala's head pop up like a cork in the river. She was moving fast.

Willis urged his body to dive as his will held him back. Then he threw his arms forward and plunged in.

His clothes tangled around his limbs, dragging him down and spinning him into a somersault against his will. The current dragged his head below the surface and he caught a fuzzy glimpse of thousands of bubbles, ever-darker deep green water to one side and the pale green and white light that was the surface to the other.

His nose filled with water, his fingers brushed against slimy rocks, and he thrashed his way towards the light and shook his wet hair out of his eyes.

He glimpsed Sala's head and arms splashing before she was swept around a bend in the river. He beat his arms and legs together, trying to raise himself higher out of the water, his clothes weighing him down. He got out one shout over the roar of the river before choking on a mouth full of water.

Sala's head jerked around - it may have been in response, or she may just have been swimming. Willis decided to save his own energy and concentrate on staying afloat.

Then the river - and the landscape it was in - changed. Everything seemed to tip, like a table being lifted at one end. The water surface remained flat, like a slow-moving river, or a still lake, but sloped. Everything was flowing downhill, fast. Willis felt more like he was on a ski run, or a toboggan hurtling down a hill.

He lay back as if he were in a luge, his legs floating in front of him, using his arms to paddle and steer himself through the currents. Sometimes the water was only a few inches deep and he felt himself sliding and skipping over slippery rocks covered with algae.

He could tell where the water was moving faster and slower – by the shore there were dead spots, with eddies slowly spinning little vortexes. He approached a narrow spot, where the water ran fast and deep, and he bodysurfed through it between a rocky peninsula and a reddish-orange boulder.

He sailed down hills like this, through shallows and deep, the pine trees on shore whizzing by, the water weirdly flat and consistent.

Then he was shooting towards the edge of a waterfall. He tried to back-paddle, but soared over the edge and found himself sliding down a steep 200-foot long slope, sliding over rocks in turbulent water maybe six inches deep.

At the bottom of the slope was a bowl-shaped lake, green at the edges and deep blue in its centre. It looked like a cup being held by a stone hand, gently tipping the water out to the left. There was a dark smooth rippling edge where the water disappeared.

The fingers of stone hand gripping the bowl of the lake extended out in a cliff of yellow stone, streaked with red granite. It jutted over a flat plain - hundreds or thousands of feet below – that extended to purple hills on the horizon.

On the side farthest from the falls the water was shallowest, its colour lightening to a pale yellow-green. At the edge of the water, Willis could see Sala dragging herself ashore.

The sun was beating down on the rock and the water in the shallows was soup-warm.

It was only when he stood clear of the water that Willis realized how tired he was. His legs almost gave way, his soaking clothes feeling as if he were draped in sheets of lead.

He dropped back down to all fours and dragged himself onto the rock, collapsing near Sala, who looked like a tangled wet rag. Both gasping for breath, they said nothing. Willis lay there, feeling the rock radiating heat through his wet clothes and warming his back.

Eyes closed, Willis caught his breath, watching the swirling patterns of blurry cobwebs and abstract shapes of red illuminated by the sun on his eyelids.

He heard the scuff of a footstep on rock, and the glowing red he saw went black.

CHAPTER 5
DUST

SOMEONE WAS STANDING in his light. Willis looked up and saw the outline of an athletic young woman standing above him. He sat up quickly.

"Are you alright?" she said, extending a hand to help him up. She heaved him to his feet without an effort, and gave him an open smile.

Willis felt dizzy. He was quite sure no one this beautiful had ever looked him in the face before, and he couldn't remember anyone looking that happy to see him. He didn't know anyone could have that many teeth, so white and so perfectly shaped. She was a few years older than him - a senior in High School, maybe? Older?

She was wearing rock-climbing gear, with a coil of rope on one hip and a belt covered in clips and equipment. He couldn't see her eyes, because she was wearing wraparound sunglasses with a rainbow hue, like oil on water.

"I'm Maya. You're not from around here are you?"

"No - I..." Sala let out a little moan and rocked her head.

"Let me just check on my friend," Willis knelt and touched his fingers to Sala's throat to check her pulse. She had one, anyway. He patted her cheek, which was cool, because her body was still holding the temperature of the cold water. Her eyes fluttered but didn't open. She gulped awkwardly, without saying anything, her mouth slack, but gulping like a pouting goldfish.

Maya stepped over him. "I think she's going

to be sick. Help me turn her over." She deftly rolled Sala onto her side, supporting her head and shifting Sala's knee as Willis moved awkwardly around.

As soon as she was over on her side, Sala retched and vomited up clear water as if they had overturned a jug - once, twice, then stopped. She took a deep breath, an unconscious sigh of relief, then settled back into stillness.

"I think she'll be all right," Maya said. "How did you get up here?"

"We came down that," said Willis, pointing up the strange slope of water.

Maya stood relaxed with a hand on her hip. Her smile stretched slowly into a knowing, gently mocking look. "You really aren't from around here then,"

Willis couldn't take her eyes off her. She was a mischievous cat, relaxed but brimming with energy, about to pounce. In the face of her inexhaustible calm, Willis felt humbled, almost belittled. A ripple of exhaustion ran through his frame and the rumpled, still-heavy, half-damp clothes he was wearing started to itch in weird places - behind his knees, down his back.

"No, I'm not from around here," he passed his hand over his eyes and lurched forward to catch himself, as the ground heaved under him like the deck of a ship on heavy seas. He lowered himself to the rock and sat down heavily.

"Are you ok?" Maya asked, squatting down in front of him and peering at his face.

"I just - I wish I could find a short cut." He pressed his hands against his closed eyes, seeing spirals and jets of fluorescent squares.

"A short cut?" Maya said. "You're a dreamer."

"Am I asking that much?" Willis asked. "Is it that impossible?"

"No, I mean I've seen people like you before. You're a dreamer," Maya said.

She twisted back and whistled. Willis glanced up and saw three others - dressed in climbing gear, like she was, emerge from behind the rocks across the lake, waving in response.

The horizon tilted again, like being on a floating raft that's tipping because too many people are climbing on to one side. Willis thought it was dizziness, a sign he was going to pass out. But the horizon stayed tilted - and the water in the lake in front of him started to slosh sideways, like soup in a bowl. The world was turning upside down, and they were all being tipped toward the edge of the cliff.

Maya calmly started to hammer pitons into the rock, deftly looping rope through anchors, tying subtle knots. Then she'd move a few feet over, tapping in another hold.

"What's happening?" he said.

Maya didn't look up from her hammering.

"Come with us," she said.

Willis turned back to Sala, whose body was swaying slightly. The world tipped again and Sala's limp leg flipped straight, the rubber toe of her shoe skipping downwards in little scuds along the rock.

"I have to take Sala with me," said Willis.

The ground shifted again under his feet and he crabwalked down towards her limp form.

Maya's fellow climbers had built a virtual bridge with rope and were closing the distance fast. The knot in Willis' stomach tightened, not just from the landscape spinning. The way the other climbers were moving together was creepily synchronized. Their arms and legs were splayed but moving in perfect coordination with one another, like the legs of a giant bug. There was something weirdly off-putting about it.

Maya turned her head to look back at Sala. "She can come with us," she said.

Willis said nothing, but a voice in his head was repeating no, no and no. The lake in front of him was pouring out in an ever-widening waterfall. The "slide" he had come down had great gouts of water spilling down it, in crashing waves six feet high.

The cliff they were on kept tipping closer to vertical. Willis put himself between the edge and Sala, crouching down and trying to grab her, but wasn't sure what to do. He tried to sling her arm over his shoulders, or carry her across his back fireman-style, but she was a limp dead weight. The whole world tipped again, in a lurch and water flowing into the bowl from above sluiced across him in a curtain, knocking him to the ground and washing him and Sala closer to the edge.

He was soaking wet and slippery. They had been washed out towards the tip of the cliff, which was a couple of yards behind him. The water from above was now dropping in a sheet behind them, away into oblivion.

Willis scrambled to regain his footing, slipping towards the edge. Instead of helping Sala to her feet he was only dragging her further down.

He glanced up the slope to see Maya standing there - a rope clipped to the ground in front of her, leaning back relaxed and letting it bear her weight. She exuded confidence, and extended her hand back to Willis just as her team of co-climbers arrived, lowering themselves with military precision to the point next to her. They were all male, and all had the same wraparound sunglasses with an oily rainbow sheen.

The landscape shifted again. Willis and Maya slipped back over the rock, as Maya and her team adjusted their stances.

"Just pass her to us," one of them said, sounding impatient. Maya made a gesture that implied silence. There was something very wrong.

Willis' mind started to seize up. A glance behind him showed a sloping plain, hundreds of feet below. If he clambered down and over the edge he might be able to escape Maya, but there was nothing he could do to get Sala away. Then there was a spark of remembrance. This was just a dream. He could get out of it and get back in. He just had to wake up.

"Will you keep her safe?" he said.

Maya looked at him. She didn't seem to understand the question at all. The cliff side lurched and Willis skidded back again. He was leaning against the surface of the rock, trying to push and roll Sala's limp body upwards. One of the men released a catch on his rope, leaned back and effortlessly grabbed Sala's arm. He hauled her upwards, passing her with one arm to his team, who seized on her, attaching clips and ropes to her, spinning her like a spider wrapping its prey.

Friction alone was keeping Willis on the tipping cliff face, and he was sliding in painful skips and jerks towards the edge. Then the world tipped again and Willis was thrown off into the void.

The world tumbled into chaos around him. All he could see was spinning streaks of blue sky, dark green land, sun, white spray of water. All he could hear was the deep roar of wind and his clothes flapping and rattling.

Then the pitch of the roar shifted and started to get higher, like the gurgling in a bottle that's being filled up, and he was awake, panting and panicked.

∽

He felt as if he never really did get back to sleep. He struggled with the blinds and curtain, trying to create total darkness in his room, but the light grey sky, illuminated with a red cast from the streetlights below, couldn't be shut out.

His clock had showed a digital 3:17 AM. Then 3:51. Then whenever he glanced over, skimming in and out of a dreamless sleep: 4:22, 4:53, 5:12, 5:51, 6:46.

Once awake, the rest of the day was a fog of mumbles and blurry images.

∞

So it was for the rest of the week. When he did drop off to sleep, his dreams were shallow and repetitive. He would find himself back in Grade 3, writing a simple but endless test to which he knew all the answers, or painting an endless picket fence that stretched away to the horizon on a slightly curved earth.

By the time Friday rolled around, Sala and Maya were fading and less real. On Saturday, his parents recruited him again to go see Mad Meg.

He carried the box, felt the warmth of the food. The sky was blue-black and moonless, with enough haze to fuzz out stars. There was Meg, standing like a mannequin at the window staring out into a darkened yard. A couple of the streetlights were out, leaving black spots Willis felt he should hurry through. He felt safer in the light.

Willis had been told to go right in, but he found the main floor of Meg's house blacked out. A single light from upstairs shone straight down on the staircase, illuminating the narrow carpet clamped to the stairs with metal rungs, a threadbare and grey path worn in the middle.

As he started up the stairs, a knocking started - rhythmic, metallic and loud. Was it coming from under the floor - in the walls?

It stopped for a moment, then there was a bang so loud it could have been from a gunshot. Was it from upstairs?

Willis rushed up the steps, the food and plates sloshing around in the cardboard box.

He was panting when he shouldered his way into the room, terrifying Meg, who screamed and cowered under her blanket. Willis, startled, screamed too - a high-pitched, girlish scream, which was instantly embarrassing.

Their fear dissolved into nervous laughter. Meg actually smiled and Willis saw a glimpse of the younger woman she used to be.

"Willis, what in God's name are you doing?" she said.

"What was that sound? I thought something was wrong."

"It's just the heat, for heaven's sake. It happens with the steam pipes in this old wreck." She relaxed back and heaved a sigh. "You almost gave me a heart attack. And nearly shattered my eardrums."

"I think I may have mixed up all your food as well," said Willis, trying to unpack the plates and food onto the table next to the sofa.

He had. Everything on her plate had slipped over into a snowdrift of mashed potatoes on one side of the plate, shot through with green peas, with a chicken drumstick stuck in the side.

"I'm not too hungry right now. Just leave it there," she said. "I can always eat it later."

Willis thought about that. His parents had talked about cajoling Meg to eat more.

"Are you sure?" he said. "I could get more."

"Don't trouble yourself," She heaved another sigh, and sounded very sad.

She lay on her side and curled up, drawing her blanket over her shoulder, though the room seemed warm enough. The radiator under the window was hissing away. She stared across the room at the wall, then closed her eyes.

Was she going to sleep? Should I wake her up and get her to eat? Or take this chance to sneak out? He wondered.

She opened her eyes, and they were rimmed with tears. She blinked, and one tear overflowed the corner, running over the bridge of her nose.

"He would be about your age now, you know," she said, glancing hastily over at Willis.

He didn't.

"Who?"

"My little boy. My sweet little boy, Miles," she squeezed her eyes tight and her body shook, holding in a sob. "Don't you remember him? You played together when you were young."

Willis searched his memory. He couldn't remember meeting Miles. Was she talking about Sala's Miles?

"He was a fragile child. Spent so much time sick in bed, stuck in his rotten room. His wrists thin like sticks, his eyes sunken. All he wanted to do was get outside and play with the other kids. I didn't want to hover over him. When he was well enough, I wanted to let him roam. He was so determined to ride his bike and catch up with the other kids. The joy he had, the joy on his face when he would come down that sidewalk. I would stand at that window and watch him, and the look on his face," she gulped back a laugh of joy at the memory, "so happy, so free."

Her smile faded, and the corners of her mouth

pulled down, down, down into a mask of sadness. She closed her eyes tight again, tears rolling, then her features shifted into a look of hatred and anger.

"Then that wicked creature took him away," she said, in a voice Willis strained to hear.

"Who?"

"Sala. That little friend of his he talked about all the time."

Willis felt the hair on the back of his neck stand up and his heart started beating hard in his chest.

"Who is Sala?"

"She's a wicked creature, a wicked thing. I don't know what she is. A demon or a trickster or a banshee. A faerie who lured my little boy away." She covered her face with her arm, as if she were ashamed, then blew her nose.

"Please don't tell anyone what I've told you. I know it sounds mad. Utterly mad. I loved him so much. He's gone and all I have to blame are fairy tales. There is such a hole in my life and nothing fills it."

She wiped her nose again, and seemed to calm down.

"For a while I'd see him in dreams. He would come back to me, and I would stand at the window and watch him play. I would make him lunch and he would tell me about his day. I would be asking myself, why am I doing this? I know he's gone - but he's here. He's home now. And then I would wake up, and find myself back in the world without him. And I hated being awake in this crummy world. All I wanted to do is go back to sleep, so I could see him again.

"Then he stopped coming. But sometimes in the middle of the night, I thought I heard him calling for me. Then that stopped too."

It was quiet for a moment. Willis heard the uneven whistling of the steam radiator, then the deeper roar of a gust of wind outside.

Meg stared, glassy-eyed, blinked twice, then focused. "I'm sorry Willis. I shouldn't unburden myself on you like this. This must all seem impossible to believe. All my ravings."

Willis smiled a crooked half-smile. "It's ok." He didn't know what else to say. She looked at him intently, her eyes darting back and forth across his features. Then she seemed to fade again and her eyes took on a thousand-yard stare.

"You should get home. It's late and your parents will be worried."

"Don't forget to eat some of the dinner," Willis said. "Even all mixed together it's good. That's how my dad always eats it, anyway."

She didn't answer. She rolled over and faced the back of the couch, turning her back to him.

∽

Willis lay in bed that night, staring at the ceiling, his mind roiling. A distorted rectangle of bluish light flashed onto the ceiling, twisting and stretching itself – the headlights of a car outside turning around.

Miles was real, and was Mad Meg's son. What did she mean Sala was a Faerie, or a demon? What had really happened to Miles? He had to get back. He twisted and turned, unable to relax. His legs were full of twitches, then he felt like he was sitting in front of a campfire on a cold night - one side of his body hot, the other covered in cold sweat.

He got up and sat in his uncomfortable desk chair to read until his eyelids were heavy and drooping. He clicked off his light and slumped back to bed, but found himself getting more alert the longer he lay there. The last time he remembered looking at the clock it was past three.

He skimmed in and out of sleep past sunrise. It was Sunday, so his parents let him sleep in. He finally got comfortable sleeping face down, supported by a mountain range of crumpled pillows and blankets. The sun through the window was warm on the side of his face. His body at last lost all traces of tension, and sweating slightly, he dozed off.

The sun grew hotter and hotter on the back of his head. He felt a little thirsty but couldn't bring himself to get up.

He licked his lips to wet them. His tongue was dry and sticky and stuttered over his lips, which were chapped and flaking. He tried to swallow, but his tongue stuck to the roof of his mouth. He lifted his head and peeled open his eyes.

He was lying on flat hard yellow clay, riven with cracks a quarter inch wide, like wrinkles in an elephant's hide. They extended away as far as he could see, before the lines blurred out in the shimmering heat.

He stood up, patting the fine powdery dust off his clothes. The world was two colours: blue sky and yellow earth. He turned slowly, looking for anything that stood out on the featureless plain. It took a moment before he could start picking out details.

There were patches of shimmering mirage, a black line of horizon. Then two or three objects travelling fast in the distance. One trailing a billowing cloud of dust behind it. Ahead of it, two black dots hovering above the ground, speeding along the horizon. The dots blurred out in the haze, but the dust cloud seemed to be getting closer.

It looked like it could be a road, so Willis started walking towards it.

It was a long slog. Panting or breathing out of his mouth seemed to make him thirstier, so he sealed his lips, breathed through his nose and kept a steady pace.

An irregular black line slowly appeared, hovering over the horizon in an empty space - a line of trees. It took a while to reach them, but when he did, they were clustered around a railroad track and a parched cracked asphalt road. The road's surface was writhing with aging black veins of tar. Between the road and rail ran a ditch, with cracked mud at the bottom and a few wisps of tinder-dry grass.

Willis walked towards the trees to get some shade, sitting down heavily with his back against the gnarled trunk, edging himself around to get the most out of the shadow.

He heard the whine of a motor being pushed

to its limit, and looked down the road and saw nothing - then caught a glimpse of a shape fluttering between the tree trunks, hurtling down the railroad track. It was a motorcycle, and as it came closer he saw that it had no tires. Its wheels had been modified so that its steel rims were running right on the rails, spitting out the odd spark.

The rider was crouched low on the seat, leather-clad with a black helmet and visor that let you see nothing of his or her face, like a black beetle clinging to a stick. In fact, there were two of them.

They shot past, the pitch of their engines dropping dramatically as they roared by. Willis stood up to get a clear view, following them with his eyes until they disappeared in the ripples of the heat rising from the desert floor.

⟨⟩

He was intent on them, and didn't hear the gurgling rumble of the truck coming up behind him on the road until it almost ran him over. He jumped aside and backed off into the trees, but it pulled to a stop with a screech, and three young men jumped out, tackling him and dragging him to the back of the truck, which was covered by a yellowing duct-taped cap.

Willis struggled and kicked, but they had a solid grip on his ankles. They rolled him into the back and slammed the tailgate shut so loud his ears rang. He was tossed sideways as the truck fishtailed with a lurch and peeled down the road.

In moments they were clear of the trees, accelerating constantly until they hit a cruising speed. It smelled of solvents, gas, oil and rust. He could hear the muffled shouts of the passengers screaming over the engine's roar, though he couldn't make out anything they said. There were rust holes in the floor of the cab through which he could see a blur of asphalt, and at every pothole or dip in the road, everything in the back would jump and slide around. A screwdriver, nuts and bolts, a length of chain, a tow rope with a sturdy, rust-covered hook on it, gerry cans of gasoline and a fair-sized boat anchor, also covered in rust.

He looked through the grease-smudged window to the cab. The guy in the middle was pointing out the window and jabbing his finger, while the one sitting closest to the door nodded his head, and rolled down the passenger side window.

Then he climbed out, using the side mirror as a grip, and lowered himself to the road, glancing up and down at his feet. Then he let go of the mirror, and shot past the side window, standing up.

He was holding some kind of tow rope, and standing what looked like a steel skateboard, leaning back and cutting back and forth on the road as if he were water skiing. The board sent up showers of sparks and black gravel, tearing up a long s-shaped scar down the middle of the highway.

Willis watched in amazement, expecting the man to tumble at any moment. If anything went wrong he would have his skin scuffed off in a matter of moments.

The young man could see that Willis was watching. His mouth spread into a gloating smile with teeth that shone white against his tanned skin. Willis must have scowled, but the man, still smiling, let go of the tow rope with one hand and pointed away from the road. They were passing a water tower with the word SMILE on it.

Then the roadsurfer started to weave back and forth across the road in ever-greater arcs, so he was sometimes nearly passing the truck, or driving alongside it. He made a hand gesture so the truck pulled over to the middle of the road and he pulled into place next to the passenger door, lifted himself from the road and hoisted himself into the truck.

Willis shook his head. Then he had a sense of déjà vu. They were passing exactly the same water tower - a squat tin can on spindly steel legs painted all white, except this time it said LIMES.

Maybe the fumes from the gas are getting to me back here, he thought.

Out of the corner of his eye he caught a commotion in the cab of the truck. A couple of the young men were changing places, climbing over each other, and the one who had been sitting in the middle was climbing out the passenger window and lowering himself to the road.

He, too, started roadsurfing, pulling off flips and tricks, the blackened asphalt gravel spraying like the foam on a whitecap. Then again, another water tower. This time it said SELIM.

Smile, limes, selim. They all had the same letters. What if you rearranged them or read them backwards?

Smile was elims.

Limes was semil.

Selim backwards was Miles.

He had to get to one of those watertowers.

The middle man was hauling himself in towards the truck as Willis threaded the rope through the loop of the anchor. The anchor was heavy, but surprisingly well-balanced, like an axe or a hammer. He opened the window at the back of the cab and looked down. The truck had a hitch, and the hook on the rope would just fit around the narrowest part. He dropped the hook around it.

Willis lowered the gate, which dropped with a bang, and crawled out onto it on his knees, dragging the anchor.

The wind over the top of the truck buffeted him, nearly blowing him onto the road. Steadying himself as best as he could, with the truck hurtling down the highway, he swung the anchor down as if he were splitting a log.

The anchor bit and embedded in the road, the rope unfurled behind him in a flash. In a second it was taut, and the truck was slowed as if it had hit a wall. Willis was thrown forward, somersaulting back into the cab.

The truck stopped. Willis suddenly realized how stupid his plan had been, and how lucky he was. The anchor might well have boomeranged back into the back of the truck like a slingshot.

He scrambled out on all fours, dropped to

the pavement and started running for the nearest water tower. It seemed to take forever. The distance was deceiving: the tower was actually huge, though it had looked smaller - and closer - before. He could hear the men shouting for him, but he remembered something from running track - don't turn around to check, it will slow you down too much.

His legs felt rubbery but he closed the distance quickly. Two of the men were chasing him. Where was the third?

The clay ground was hard on his feet, then he grabbed the ladder and was climbing straight up on the flat iron rungs. The muscles in his legs were burning as he climbed through a grated hatchway, then ran around a catwalk and sprinted, exhausted, up two flights of stairs to find himself staring at a hatchcover, topped with a wheel to open it. He could hear the clanging of footsteps below him as he twisted the wheel, which was stiff and squealed in protest.

Then the hatch was open and he was staring

down into the tank. He caught the whiff of cool water with a hint of chlorine. There - at the bottom of the tank - was a circle of yellow-green light, mottled and rippling. It wasn't coming from the hatch he had opened - it looked as if there were a window at the bottom into another, watery world.

He heard footsteps on the stairs now, just below him. Still panting from his run, he took a couple of breaths to calm down and fill his lungs, then stepped through the hatchway and dove towards the light at the bottom.

The water was cool, not cold. Its temperature wasn't a shock, but its very wetness was. Willis could feel his parched body soaking up the water like a sponge, as he kicked and fought his way to the bottom of the tank. He could feel the pressure growing as he swam deeper. One of his ears popped painfully, and still his progress was slow. He fought the urge to swim back to the top, but his breathing reflex was redoubling itself.

Now he was only a few feet away from the

bottom. All he could see was a yellowy-green blur, and his other ear popped from the pressure. It was a circular hole in the bottom of the tank, two and a half feet across. Through it, Willis could see shapes that looked like the algae-covered rocks in a stream, dappled by sunlight shining through waves. He grabbed the sides of the hole and pulled himself through.

He flopped out like a fish being poured out of a bucket, landing in a shallow pool in near total-darkness. He stood up, stumbling on rounded rocks covered in slime, and half-paddled his way to the edge of the water.

He was standing in a cave, totally enclosed, with the echoing roar of running water. Behind him was the hole he had come from, gushing water into the pool, which streamed forward past his feet.

His eyes adjusted slowly to the dark. The first thing he could make out were greenish bubbles fizzing in the water. The rocks, too, were greenish black.

He felt his way forward, bracing himself against the walls of the cave for balance, trying to keep one hand in front of his face so he didn't walk straight into an outcropping.

There was light coming from somewhere off to the right. He stumbled and splashed a few feet further, then saw water gushing out through a hole a bit wider than his own body, at about shoulder height. Through the wavering surface of the water he could see something pale green and glowing.

There was no knowing what it was, but it was the closest thing to an escape that Willis could see. He felt his way around. the rock, feeling for handholds. The rock hadn't been worn smooth by the water - there were ridges and lumps. He pulled himself into the stream and started pushing himself against the current.

It was a strange feeling, climbing against the current, but not as impossible as he had worried it might be. The sound was a muffled roar of gurgles and bubbles as he climbed toward the pale green light, which was growing steadily brighter. He held tight with his hands and tried to use his legs to push himself forward and up.

He could see what looked like sky beyond, wavering and distorted by waves on the surface. It was a bottleneck, and though he could squeeze his head and one arm through the hole, his torso and ribs were wedged painfully against the sides of the rock.

His lungs were already on fire from holding his breath, choking back the urge to panic. If he let go now, he would be swept back down to cavern to start over. If he kept going, he might just get stuck, unable to move up or down. But the surface was so close.

He braced himself, securing foot- and handholds, and expelled all the air from his lungs, watching his last breath storm up to the surface in a torrent of bubbles. He started forcing himself upwards, and the slime-covered rock scraped hard against his chest. For a moment he was pinned and felt as if the stones were pressing against his chest. He crushed out a few more bubbles from his lungs and bore down, dragging himself through the gap as the stone ground against his chest.

Then he was through, kicking and pushing his way to the top. There was a creeping darkness at the edge of his vision, and he took a great gulp of air as he breached the surface, flailing his arms to get to the shallows. He crawled on his hands and knees over the round stones, flopping down, gasping. He lay there for a moment, letting the oxygen seep back into his tingling fingers and feet.

Then he was conscious of the throbbing in his chest, made worse when he took an especially deep breath. He rolled over and looked down at his chest. There was a long red stain, pink at the edges, on his shirt. He lifted the collar and the skin stung as he pulled it away from the wound. It was one of those scrapes that felt a lot worse than it looked.

Looking around, he found himself at the

bottom of a sinkhole, sixty feet across, and thirty feet deep, ringed with blobby black rocks that looked like frozen waterfalls. There were trickles of water over the lip and a few shallow pools. There was a tree not far away, blackened and dead. The sky was a patchy grey of low clouds, so he couldn't tell what time of day it was.

He had a huge involuntary shiver, like a dog shaking itself off. He looked at his fingertips, which were all puckered, and saw they were trembling. He had gone from baking in dry heat to being cold and soaking wet.

He sat there for a while, water running down his face and dripping steadily off his nose, shivering. Was it getting darker? Willis heaved himself to his feet, his arms and legs sore, and tried to warm himself, shaking the stiffness out of his limbs. There was a wide crevasse in one of the cliff walls where the stones looked climbable, and he started to pick his way up.

The climbing was easier than it first looked. The stones were sure and solid beneath his feet, and edges gave him ready handholds. He hauled himself over the edge.

He was standing on a plain, pockmarked with ponds and rounded islands that rose out of the ground like a whale's back, or standing waves. The rock was crusted with blue and green lichen or topped with little scrub brush.

He was overlooking an even larger sinkhole - like a hammer strike into soft wood, or a cane into mud - only it was a mile wide, rimmed with waterfalls around its entire circumference. The other side was so far away it was fading into a blue haze. He walked towards the edge.

The sun peeked out at the edge of the sky. He watched the patches of sun and shadows of cloud drifting across the bottom of the crater. In the very centre was a round black lake, with a network of streams and tributaries leading to it from every direction. From directly above, Willis realized the crater would look like an eye: the black lake as a pupil, surrounded by a patchwork of green lichen, grey stone and blue water that was the iris. The ground around the lake was stained black, fading to stronger colours at the edge.

At the lake's edge, there was a spindly grey pier, extending far out into the water. Walking to the edge of the falls, Willis looked down and saw that a rock fall provided a way down. He was in no rush to get down to the bottom, and picked his way down.

It took him long enough that by the time he reached the bottom the sun was starting to set. It was darker already in the sinkhole, but the clouds at one end of the sky were a reddish-purple.

He picked his way towards the pier, walking over the little granite islands and leaping over the water that ran between them. He saw a series of lanterns being lit along the length of the pier, a flickering flame hovering between each one, then glowing alive.

He reached flatter ground - it was dry and matte black, like burned wood, or the soot in a chimney. The pier was clear to him now: young trees strapped together with planks in a rough bridge that looked both elegant and fragile. He saw movement around the steps on the shore and stopped.

It was quiet, so quiet now. He could hear his heart beating and his pulse in his ears. The sound of their feet clunking on the wooden steps carried to him clear across the water. It was Sala and Maya. He could recognize Sala's birdlike frame and her light step. Maya's movements were graceful and smooth, like a dancer. Despite the near complete darkness, Maya was still wearing her sunglasses. There were two other people with them, carrying torches.

They walked the length of the pier, past the suspended lanterns that threw soft yellow-orange pools of light on the deck, and started to walk down another set of stairs that took them right into the water.

He could see them walking in, following the steps down, but when they reached the oily lake, they just kept going down, as if they were hypnotized. The water closed over their heads, like crude oil, and swallowed them up. There was barely a ripple to show they had been there.

Willis crept up to the steps and tiptoed up. The silence was almost oppressive.

He reached the top of the stairs. The pier – a crooked path of rough-hewn boards, all of three feet wide and illuminated by round paper lanterns - seemed suspended in space, between black sky and black water.

He jogged along the creaking boards towards the end. Here, two final lanterns illuminated the steps down into the lake. He could see their dim reflection on the slow-rolling surface.

He crept down towards the lake. He tested the liquid, feeling with his foot for the first submerged step. Instead of flowing like water, the lake oozed around his foot like molasses, slightly warm. He took another step. Yes, the railing and stairs just kept going down.

He kept stepping in, carefully, until the lake was up near his armpits.

If Maya and Sala had gone in, he must be able to as well.

He kept stepping down, keeping his mouth and nose above the water as long as he could. He was on tiptoe and his mouth was teetering above the slick black liquid.

It was time to take the plunge. He took one last breath and ducked his head beneath the surface, and everything went white.

Chapter 6
Light

WILLIS WAS IN A CROWD. Not just any crowd. The biggest one he'd ever been in. Bodies were packed tight like the audience at a rock concert, jostling back and forth. The talk of the crowd was continual roar, sometimes shifting in pitch and volume like crashing waves in a storm.

Willis couldn't see what was going on. He tried to jump a little to see how far the crowd went - just as the people around him smushed together. The crowd carried him, his arms pinned up against his chest, twitching feebly like a T. Rex, his toes dragging across the ground. He caught a glimpse between the heads and shoulders around him, and all he saw was the crowd, extending out to the horizon, bodies heaving back and forth in ocean waves, or gusts of wind on a field of grain.

Then everyone spaced out a little - at least enough for the crowd to loosen its grip on him and let him drop down to his feet. He worried for a moment he would fall and be trampled, but there wasn't even room for him to do that.

Hemmed in, he craned his neck around. How would he ever find Sala and Maya - to say nothing of Miles?

But how could they get anywhere in this crowd? Maybe he could just go with the flow, he thought, then was shoved and dragged four feet to his left, then pushed and dragged another three feet back and to the side.

Well, he thought. This isn't working. The air around him was stale and moist. He looked into the faces of the people around him. It was hard to catch a glimpse of their features. They all seemed to be adults, mostly facing the same direction as him. A man turned his head, looking around. The thing that struck Willis was the intensity of the man's expression, coupled with a blind, unfocused look in his eyes. Then he was shoved again from behind, hard.

The crowd relaxed again and the space between everyone grew. Willis decided to plant his feet and get his elbows up. He remembered from somewhere that if you made a fist and turned your middle finger into a little pointy triangle, you could jab it into people's ribs and they would find it uncomfortable.

So every time he was shoved, he would give the person crushed against him a good pinch. He started stepping on toes, and when space allowed he'd get a good kick in. He never had to bite.

His little battle seemed to working. Aside from the shuffling and stamping of a million feet, and the incoherent shouting and talk, he managed to elicit some yips and grunts of discomfort and pain. The space started clearing just a little more. He felt a gust of cooler, cleaner air waft over him and gulped at it.

The crowd was milling, too, and he moved into what was a clearer space. A man was in front of him, over six feet tall, was jostled by the crowd, and stepped back onto Willis' foot, his heel pinning and grinding two of his toes. Angry, Willis aimed a kick at the back of one of his knees, thinking for a moment he might bring the man down.

The kick made the man waver and stumble, and he turned slowly to face Willis. He fixed himself in the stance of a gunslinger, feet apart, arms relaxed at his sides, ready for a showdown. His expression was so hard to read, Willis couldn't tell if he was angry or just stupid. Or worse, both. But he was very tall and fit. He settled into this position and stared down at Willis, still as a statue.

Everyone else also stopped moving, and the people around Willis and turned their bodies to face them. They cleared a space about 12 feet across, with Willis at one end and the man at the other. The roar of the crowd faded to total silence.

Oh my God, thought Willis. If he wants to fight I'm dead.

Now, everywhere Willis looked, eyes were on him. Hundreds - thousands of pairs of eyes - looking at him. The man - his opponent? - slowly raised his arm, pointing an accusing finger at Willis. Then he opened his mouth and his features drooped, and he made a noise - a low, moaning keen, accompanied by a slack-featured look of horror. He was scared of Willis.

The side of the circle opened up as people stepped back and created an open space - a pathway, with people on either side lined with military precision like soldiers on parade. Down that aisle walked Maya, draped in a white outfit that caressed the ground as she walked up. Sala was walking behind her, looking miserable.

"A disturbance," Maya said, walking up to

Willis. She looked serious, but not unfriendly.

"I thought I was going to be crushed," said Willis. Did Maya not recognize him? Sala must, but she wouldn't raise her eyes to look at him.

"You are upsetting us by being so separate. Aren't you terribly alone?"

"No," Willis said, without really thinking. Then he wondered whether that was true.

There were times he felt very alone, when he felt low and needed someone to talk to. He loved his parents, but they were busy and it often was hard to explain why he felt bad. Sometimes when he did he felt silly, as if he were complaining about nothing. It always seemed to be at those times that he couldn't get a hold of his friends.

"At least, not really," he added.

"Why don't you stay here with us? You could be part of something greater, instead of a little thing all alone," said Maya.

Willis thought about the mad bustle of the crowd. "Just moments ago I was fighting for space," he said.

"But look at it now," said Maya, gesturing to the crowd. There was an incredible silence and stillness. Willis shifted and could hear his clothes scuffing against each other.

"And it doesn't have to be like this." She lifted her hand and parts of the crowd started to clear, while others ran and swirled together like a flock of birds, then they all lay down, in a never-ending spiral with their feet facing towards the three figures who were still standing: Maya, Sala and Willis.

Maya gestured out over her people with a grand sweep of her arm, effortlessly graceful like a ballerina, "Here we are all bound together, part of the whole. We share together. We feel together. We grieve together. We love together. We dream together."

"But this is all a dream, my dream," said Willis.

"Are you so certain?" Maya pressed closer to him. She was incredibly beautiful and elegant. "Are you dreaming me? Are you dreaming all this? Or are we dreaming you? If this girl can be part of your dream, yet real, why can't you be part of the dream too? Who is dreaming who?"

Willis' head spun. He tried to come up with a reason or recall something that he could offer as proof of a time he knew he was dreaming, or when it was real, but everything seemed slippery and impossible to grasp.

He scrubbed his face with his hands. Was Sala working for Maya? Had she been trying to lure him down to this level all along? Willis closed his eyes and riffled through his memories, like a stack of old photos, trying to hold on to something real. There was so much weird he had to sort through – the dreams with water and deserts, falling and climbing.

Then he thought of his parents - not the phony ones in the dream-airport. His real ones. At the diner on the highway.

He recalled it as if he had been dropped into the restaurant. There was his dad, sitting across from him at a chocolate-brown fake wood table, in a maroon-coloured booth with vinyl seats, looking out at the highway, a bleached postcard of washed-out colours in the noonday sun. He remembered the taste of that cola, sweet and fizzing on his tongue, perfect square ice cubes with a round hole in the middle you could stick your straw through, jingling in the top of the glass. The smell of vinegar and grease wafting off his dad's scalding-hot french fries, the tiny crunch of the crust on the hamburger bun, which had been toasted on the grill. The chopped onions that he hated but the cook had put in anyway by accident, and that his mom scraped out onto his plate. And next to Willis sat Sala, giving him that look where most of her face looked sweet and innocent but her eyes were laughing and filled with mischief.

He looked up at Maya and Sala.

"I remember eating lunch with my dad. At a Diner, when I was kid. That was real."

Maya turned and looked slyly back at Sala.

"Was she there?" Maya asked, tipping her

head back toward Sala. A cryptic smile was tugging up the corner of her mouth.

Willis opened his mouth to answer and froze. Why was Maya asking that? How could she know? He felt that if he answered honestly, and said yes, that Sala might get in trouble. Something inside him urged him to lie. He choked it down.

"Yeah, she was," he said.

"So the only 'real' memory you can recall is one that has an 'imaginary friend' in it?" Maya asked.

"My dad was there," said Willis.

"Your dad. But if it was half real and half imaginary, how do you know which half?"

"It was real," Willis said.

Maya stepped very close. The entire crowd was silent and so motionless they might as well have been a forest of statues on a windless day.

"Your little friend here - what's her name, Sala? Is she real?"

Willis looked at Sala, looking miserable, her skin pale and dark smudges under her eyes.

He looked at her, so sad. Then he thought of Miles and what Meg had said about Sala: that she was a faerie, or a witch who had stolen her boy away. He looked at her, wondering exactly why she looked so sad, but her face was closed to him.

Was she sorry for what she had done? Or was she sorry for herself? Sorry for what had happened to Miles, and for tricking him, Willis? Or just guilty that she had to stand there and watch, knowing what Maya was about to do, playing with him like a cat with a mouse?

He made up his mind. He was going to say the thing that would make Maya mad.

"I don't know what she is," Willis said. "But she is my friend."

Whatever answer Maya had been hoping for, this wasn't it. Her smile vanished and the crowd erupted in a chaotic gabbling incoherent roar. There was a crack in the military-style formation as a shudder of reaction ran through the crowd, rippling like a wave down the aisle that had opened up for Maya's arrival.

Maya reached forward and grabbed Willis's hand, holding it palm up and pulling it forward in a steely grip, prying open his fingers with her thumb. She lifted her other hand high, and brought it down in a fist in the middle of Willis' palm. He felt an agonizing and sharp pain - a needle driven deep into his hand.

The crowd went silent again, like someone had pulled the plug of a headphone jack. The only sound he heard was a high pitched tone, like ringing in his ears slowly getting louder.

Willis struggled to pull his hand loose, but Maya's hand was locked to his. When he yanked it back it sent an agonizing pain that paralysed his hand, and sent a live wire of pulsing electric pain from his palm clear to his shoulder.

It hurt so much Willis was afraid to move. He stood frozen, then realized that aside from the pain, he couldn't feel his arm at all. Numbness was spreading across his chest, preceded by a tingling feeling like crawling insects, that left everything behind it feeling cold and dead.

The frozen feeling was spreading up to his face. He tried to speak but his lips felt thick and rubbery, then the blankness crossed his eyes. The scene blurred and faded to white.

CHAPTER 7
DARK

WILLIS FELT WARM and sleepy, wrapped up tight like a mummy. His arms were close around his body. His legs may or not have been crossed. He couldn't tell. Were his arms folded? Which was his right hand and which was his left?

It was bright and he drifted in and out of consciousness, his eyes fluttering open to a creamy light yellow, the colour of white chocolate. Sometimes he would see shapes and outlines - a vague horizon. He didn't have the energy to look about, so he just stared up at the white walls and ceiling - or was it the sky? The blank whiteness would start to eat away and dissolve the details, swallowing them up. Then his eyes would flutter closed again.

All around him he could hear a constant murmuring, the insistent chatter of thousands of people. He strained to pick out single voices but still couldn't understand any words, just a jabber of syllables or the tail end of a laugh.

Sometimes there would be a wave of cold, and the tips of his toes would freeze and tingle, feeling prickly and painful. Then another wave of warmth, and a thaw, and his toes would hurt then almost start to itch.

He felt a mouth press against his - lips, warm and firm. He opened his eyes and saw Sala's face, her eyes closed and serious. He made a surprised grunt and she sat straight up, her ears turning very red. She wiped her mouth with the back of her hand and made a disgusted face.

"Are you awake?" she asked.

"Yes," he said. He twitched his fingers and wiggled his toes. Now he knew where everything was. His arms were crossed, and so were his legs, and his right hand was in his left armpit. He unbundled, unfolding himself like an animal after hibernation, stiff and slow. There was a thin transparent shell on him that cracked off in sheets, like a snake shedding its skin.

Sala pulled him to his feet. "Come on," she said, and started to pull him away.

The scene around him was like a bleached white version of the landscape he had left around the black lake – low oval islands, a foot high protruding from a perfectly flat surface, all covered with a smooth white surface like liquid plastic. He was lying in an indent in one of these little hills, cradled like a pea in a pod. In some of the little hills Willis could see the outline of limbs, like someone had been shrink-wrapped to their bed. On other ones it was smooth and you could barely detect the outline of a crooked arm.

"Where are we?"

"This is the lowest level. This is where they put the people who don't fit in with the collective," she said. "I followed you down."

"Slow down," said Willis. Sala didn't answer, picking her way between the smooth white mounds. Glancing down, Willis sometimes thought he could see the outline of an ear or a face. He jogged to catch up with her and caught her by the elbow, pulling her around.

"Will you cut it out? Stop jerking me around. I want to know what's going on," he said.

"I thought you said you were my friend?" Sala spun around.

"I said that mostly to make Maya mad."

"It worked."

"I know," said Willis, rubbing the sore spot in he left palm with his right thumb. "Before I go anywhere with you, I need to know why you lied to me about Miles being your brother."

She stopped. "Not so loud," she hissed.

"Who's gonna hear it?" he said, even louder.

"Shhh!" she said, looking ashamed. "How

did you know?"

"How do you think? Mad Meg - I mean, Margaret - told me. She said Miles was her boy and that you took him away. Did you?"

"No. Not exactly. Please Willis, we have to keep moving. I need to bring you to where we can find him," Sala pulled at his hand, but he dug in his heels.

"Just tell me what happened, or I'm not going anywhere. I'll just find some way to wake up."

"He was friends with me, just like you were. There was even times we all played together, in that treehouse, remember? I ate at the table with him. But he didn't like the games you and I had played. You and me, we played on the beach between our worlds, the edge between your land and my ocean. Miles would get bored and wanted to swim in the ocean and explore. I didn't know - I took him further into the dream world and he didn't always want to go back."

"Then, instead of me going to him, Miles somehow went two dreams deep on his own, and he found me. We played on the fields and swam in the river and talked and climbed trees and then he said he was bored with the same old games he could do in the real world. He said he wanted to fly, like you said you did."

"Then Maya came," she looked around furtively and lowered her voice, which was trembling with emotion. "I had never met her before. She looked just the same and she told Willis he could fly if he wanted to. And he left me and he fell," she gulped back a sob, "he fell with her into the sky."

"I tried to follow but I couldn't. I spent years looking for him, travelling up and down, peering into dreams, or swimming down here," Sala's eyes had been downcast, and now she raised them to look Willis in the eye.

"I never meant for it to happen. It was after you went away. We had been such good friends, and I was so lonely. I didn't understand. I wanted another friend like you and was afraid to lose Miles, too. And then I lost him, and his mom did too. I was just afraid that if I told you the truth you would never come with me." Willis felt terrible. Then an idea occurred to him, that gave him a sharp pang in the chest.

"Do you have a mom who's missing you too?"

"I don't know," Sala closed her eyes and two fat teardrops rolled down her cheeks. "I don't remember anymore."

The murmuring around them had gone quiet. Willis reached over and brushed the tears from her face. He had a lump in his throat.

"I understand now. Sorry I was such a jerk about it," he said.

She smiled and brushed another tear out of the way.

"Thanks," she said, hugging him quickly.

Willis wasn't sure he should return the hug. He stood for a moment with his arms sticking out like a doll, then gently patted her on the back. She stood back.

"Let's go get Miles," he said.

∽

They half-jogged through the unending field of the smooth white domes. The sky was a similar off-white and Willis could barely tell which way they were facing. For all he knew, they could have been going around in circles, but Sala kept leading him on, like a dog tracking a scent. Sometimes she would pause at a corner, count off a few domes by pointing with her finger, then take off in a new direction.

Everything seemed a little greyer - the featureless sky, the domes. Was it getting darker, or were the colours actually changing? He couldn't tell, but everything was taking on an ashy grey colour. The little domes, too, were more irregularly spaced and lower to the ground.

They slowed, and Sala's steps grew more uncertain. She would backtrack, or stop for longer. The searching was starting to wear on Willis. They stopped for a particularly long time, and he sat and was starting to feel tired and dejected.

Sala was looking around as if she had

dropped a key in a field, her eyes flicking up and down, from the middle distance to the horizon. She looked tired, too - verging on frantic.

Then Willis noticed a series of little black dots - irregular drips of ink or paint - along the ground, running in a line between Sala's feet, then curving away. It was the only thing that wasn't grey.

"What's that from?" He pointed.

"What?" she turned around.

"Right there. Between your feet."

She looked down and did a little jump, slapping her forehead in surprise.

"That's what I was looking for! Right in front of me. We're close now."

They followed the drips of black snaking around the domes until they found one that had a smear of black on the side.

"I marked it earlier," she said.

Inside an indentation on top of the dome there was the curled-up figure of a little boy lying on his side. He was covered in something like a shell, like the layers of paint on an old door.

"What do we do? Are you sure it's him?" Willis asked. Sala crouched down and looked at his face - eyes closed, mouth a little open and slack, as if he were a sculpture of a child in a deep sleep.

She made a gesture as if to smooth the hair out of Miles' eyes, running her hand tenderly over his forehead.

"It's him," she said. She bent down and kissed him gently on the temple.

Nothing.

"Is that all you have to do?" said Willis.

"Wait."

Willis felt his heart beat in the silence. There was a little hiss of exhalation from Miles' mouth, followed by a sharp intake of breath. Then the weird shell he was in started to crack, first around his torso from breathing in, then at his shoulder joints and elbows. He was stirring and struggling, so Willis bent down to help, grabbing his hand and trying to get Miles to his feet. Whatever encased him cracked and broke away like a thick egg shell, cracking in pieces big and small.

Miles squeezed his fingers tight, then opened his hand, shaking off bits of shell, before tearing at his face. The crust came away like half a mask, splitting down one cheek as the other half crumbled away.

And there was Miles, blinking furiously, trying to wake up while getting specks and crumbs out of his eyes, standing holding a mask of himself. His skin had a sweaty sheen to it, his hair was damp like a freshly-hatched bird.

He looked back and forth at Willis and Sala.

Sala was beaming at Willis, her eyes wet.

Miles stared back.

"Who are you? What am I doing here?"

"I'm Willis."

"I'm Sala. Don't you remember me?"

Miles shook his head, looking from face to face with a growing look of fear.

"Who am I?" Miles said.

A cracking sound like a dry tree branch

being snapped nearby, made them all jump. One of the bodies in a nearby pod was sitting up, and struggling to stand, its shell falling away, clawing and tearing at its chest and face to break free.

Willis took a step toward it.

"Should we help... it?" he asked.

He looked back. Sala was looking on in horror and shaking her head. Miles was staring, frightened and uncomprehending.

The thing that was emerging wasn't a trapped kid like Miles. Instead of a sheen of sweat, it was covered in some kind of black ooze, and it wasn't even human in shape - or only partly so.

"No, Willis," Sala said. "We have to move."

Another resounding crack made them jump again, this time behind them. Another figure was struggling to sit up, like a zombie from a coffin, pieces of its white shell crumbling and flaking off like plaster, spattering across the ground. Then there was cracking all around them as bodies came to life and broke out of their brittle prisons, black liquid oozing up and out, spilling onto the glossy white.

They were rising up everywhere, in every direction. Willis had no clue which way to go.

"Come on!" Sala shrieked, grabbing him and Miles by the hand. "Follow me!"

They started to run, with the creatures erupting from the ground all around them. Willis glimpsed weird deformed creatures dragging themselves out of the earth covered in what looked like crude oil.

He saw what at first looked like a woman, with long misshapen arms pulling herself free from one of the nests and was shocked to see she that her torso tapered off to a neat point, a kind of half-woman, half-bat. With her arms she started scrabbling across the ground towards them.

Some were just creatures and not human at all. There was a giant worm, black-armored like a centipede, many-jointed, writhing and as thick as a fire hydrant. It waved its blunt, eyeless bullet-shaped head around like it was trying to catch a scent, then started undulating towards them.

There were things whose front half was a hairless dog, tapering off into the body of a salamander, or fish-faced people - a gaping fishy mouth with pointy pike teeth and a slimy fish skin, pulling themselves forward on human arms while taking great rasping gasps of air.

The whole landscape was turning dark, as black ooze spilled out from the pods around the escaping creatures. Whether by reflection or some magic sympathy the sky above was growing darker too.

Willis, Sala and Miles tried to step only on the parts of the ground that were still white, dodging and weaving, taking little leaps then long ones. It was like running down a school hallway with black-and-white checkerboard floors, and only stepping on the white tiles, except the black area was always getting bigger and the white spots were shrinking away.

Sometimes Willis' foot would catch the edge of the black ooze and he would slip a little as he ran. He took a glance over his shoulder and could see a surging wave of misshapen creatures crawling forward - toad-beings, fish-beings, dog-salamanders - slipping and sliding over one another, sometimes snapping or even eating one another.

Willis' lungs were burning, his heart pounding in his chest. The muscles in his legs were starting to seize up. The gaps of white ground that he could step on and maintain his footing were closing up.

Then Miles went down.

Poor Miles. He had been running in abject terror and keeping ahead of Willis. But he had taken a bad step, and found himself sliding into the muck.

From an unhatched pod nearby something toadlike the size of a bulldog cracked its way out and lunged for Miles. Willis jumped over Miles and gave the thing a good kick, flipping it on its back, where it squirmed, unable to right itself.

Willis too slipped and fell on his back, staring for a moment up at the sky. It was growing ever-blacker - a starless charcoal grey.

Willis pulled himself, then Miles to their feet, but the creatures were circling - not just circling, but surrounding them. It was getting ever darker, and the white ground had now flooded with blackness. There was no line at the horizon dividing sky and earth, or whatever passed for sky and earth here.

The ground was black, the sky was black, and the creatures were closing in.

CHAPTER 8
FLIGHT

WILLIS, MILES AND SALA stood facing outward - they might all have been strapped to a pole, for how close they were standing.

"Sala, what do we do now?" asked Willis. She didn't answer. "Sala?"

Then she said something that was too quiet to hear.

"What did you say?" Willis shouted.

"I said I don't know," she hissed angrily.

Miles was starting to get very upset. "I can't

see!" he said. "I can't tell the difference between the ground and the sky. It's all closing in."

Miles words rang for a moment in Willis' ears. Willis stared at the ground, and then back up at the sky. He couldn't see the difference either. The sky might as well have been the ground.

Willis' head lolled suddenly and the horizon lurched. Was he dizzy? He swayed, but so had Miles and Sala - he felt them stumble along with him. This was familiar. An alarm was going off in his head.

He tried to ignore the ever-tightening circle of creatures around him and concentrate. The sky and the ground. The ground and the sky. He looked down at his feet and imagined for a moment that he was lying on his back, with his feet in the air. Nothing.

Then he looked up at the charcoal black sky above him and imagined that he was falling up into it.

The world tipped.

Everyone sloshed sideways - everyone - as the

ground beneath their feet dropped and became a 40-degree slope. The creatures downslope slipped away, leaving a dimly-visible smeared trail. Miles, Sala and Willis all collapsed in a heap, and the creatures upslope slipped towards them - though they seemed so surprised, they backpedalled to keep from slipping uncontrollably down the slope.

"Hold on, hold on!" Willis said. The three tried to pull each other upright, losing their grip on each other hands, slick with black ooze. Holding hands wasn't going to work for what he had in mind, thought Willis.

"Link arms! Link arms!" he shouted, and they scrambled together, linking arms at the elbows, with Willis in the middle.

"Wait a second." Willis concentrated - then tried to relax, half-closing his eyes to blot out distractions and the mass of writhing creatures around him. He imagined again that he was dropping into the sky - that he was at the bottom of the world, and that he was falling up.

With that, he dropped away from the ground,

and yanked Miles and Sala upwards into the sky.

They dropped together in formation, arms locked, heads back, and to Willis it didn't feel like falling. It felt like flying. He glanced past his feet and could see all the creatures, in a pillar of twisting, falling bodies and flailing limbs.

He looked back "up" in the direction he was falling - the sky - and it seemed to be lightening, ever so slightly. There was nothing to focus on, then there was a black wall only a few feet away, and an impact - not like water, like a blast of air resisting him and they were through - they had punched through the surface of the black lake from below and they dropped upwards into the sky.

The sudden shift from dark to light was blinding, and tiny muscles in Willis' eyes cramped painfully as the sun hit his face. When Willis pried his eyelids open, he, Sala and Miles were ascending in the middle of a column of swirling mist and cloud, upside-down rain and glimpses of refracted rainbows.

The whole world had turned upside down. It was as if they were at the bottom of a globe with everything pouring off it. Below them was the huge crater that Willis remembered as looking like an eye. The waterfalls around the crater's edge were running backwards, water spewing up past the cliffs in sheets. Beyond the wall of spray thrown up the sides of the crater, great clouds were swirling and forming. On one side, massive white thunderheads so imposing and firm they could have been carved from marble. On the other, clouds stained purple-grey and black, fast-moving and bubbling up in weird shapes - jagged vortexes or dripping blobs, illuminated from within by flashes of lightning.

The black lake, which had been like the eye's dark pupil, had opened up and was spilling out hundreds of those creatures - thousands - twisting now in the light. They were sickly greens and yellows, or dirty lard-white streaked with inflamed orange reds that looked infected, all smeared with that black muck. Some looked like they were starving, ribs showing and flexing as they flailed in the air. Others tried to swim through the air, flapping half-developed sickly half-wings, some tumbling pathetically or grabbing each other as if for support.

The air grew chill and damp and they passed through one cloud, then another. Willis realized then that Miles had been screaming, for quite a long time. At least since they had shot up through the surface of the black lake.

It made Willis laugh, then he tried to comfort Miles, though it was hard to be heard over the roar of their bodies tearing through the air.

"It's going to be all right!" Willis shouted, twice.

They passed into another cloud, and Willis closed his eyes against a rain squall that spattering across his face so hard it hurt. He sputtered and tried to shake it off, looking back at the ground.

Outside the towering column of flailing creatures, he could see a figure, separate from the rest. Arms and legs tucked in at her sides, poised and graceful, she plummeted past the rest and was gaining on Miles, Sala and himself.

That's Maya, thought Willis. There was something about her posture that he instantly recognized - infinitely graceful like a bird in flight. She was dropping like a falcon towards them, closing at incredible speed.

She is not just falling, he thought, she is flying.

"Hold tight!" was all he had a chance to scream when she slammed into the three of them. One of his arms was loose, and he realized he couldn't feel Sala anymore. Willis held fast onto Miles' forearm, but Sala was broken loose.

They plunged into cloud again, and as they passed through thicker and thinner patches of fog, Willis caught glimpses of Sala and Maya tumbling and fighting. Maya was clawing at her, trying to pull her closer, while Sala tried to keep her distance with kicks.

Something grabbed at his loose arm and started to shake him, shake him hard. He looked over and saw a flat, distorted fishy face, more than a foot wide, gnawing at his elbow. It had yellow eyes the size of billiard balls, needle-sharp pike teeth locking into his skin and shaking its slimy body back and forth, rattling his arm in its socket.

Willis somersaulted and shook it off, still holding tight as he could to Miles. Arcing his body he tried to take them both sideways, closer to where Maya was grappling with Sala.

He and Miles were holding each other's wrists, but Miles was twisting one way and he was twisting the other, his elbow twisting painfully, nearly dislocating his shoulder.

They floated close to Maya and Sala, who were locked in a fierce embrace. Sala's lip was split and bleeding, and she had scratches and scuffs across her face. She was fending off punches with one hand while she held onto a lock of Maya's hair with the other, pushing her face away.

Willis aimed a kick to Maya's ribs, knocking her arm away and stretching to grab for Sala's hand. They plunged through another cloud bank as Willis' hand found its mark.

When they dropped out of the fog again, Willis found himself holding Maya's arm, and Sala floating not far off. Maya swung at Willis, and started to climb his arm like a rope. He tried to shake her off, catching both feet on her shoulders, and pushed her away.

Maya spun like a lopsided starfish through space, back towards the tumbling, churning column of monsters. Twitching and wriggling, they engulfed Maya, smaller ones seizing on her arms while the rest drew her into the writhing mass.

Willis felt a shove in the back. It was Sala, grabbing hold of his free arm. They dropped into another cloud, this one dark grey, and he felt his body being pelted with ice pellets and cold mist.

Then, a lightning strike. Nearby. Even through his tightly closed eyelids, the whole world turned a dazzling white followed instantly by a crack of thunder. Crack? It was like being next to an atomic bomb, and it blew everything apart.

CHAPTER 9
HOME

WILLIS' TEETH WERE aching, his joints hurt. All he could hear was a single steady high pitched note. His nose was runny of a sudden - was it bleeding?

He was lying face down on the hard ground. He reached up to touch his lip, and found it was tacky. Half-congealed blood, with gritty black specks of dirt or sand mixed in.

He stood up. They were in the abandoned lot between Meg's house and his old place. There was no snow, but the grass was brown and packed down and the ground was hard and dry, like there had been a drought.

Willis stood up and looked around. His head ached, his ears were ringing, his nose was stuffed up with dried blood. There, nestled a dozen yards away in the crook of a leafless tree was the treehouse where he had met Sala. Close by, Miles and Sala were curled up on the ground as if they had fallen there.

Miles looked peaceful and calm, was breathing fine and seemed deep asleep. Sala's face has scratches and bruises, one eye nearly swollen shut.

Willis shook her gently by the shoulder. She groaned and rolled over.

"Are you alright?" he asked.

She sat up slowly and painfully.

"You don't have to shout. Yes, I'm OK."

"I can't hear properly. Are we back at the treehouse? I mean, the right treehouse?"

She moved her head slowly around.

"Yes. We're here."

We've been here before, the three of us, thought Willis. This is where we played.

"Can you get up?" he said.

She carefully got to her feet, limbs stiff.

"I'm a little shaky but I think I'm all right," her voice quavered. "Thanks. I've got an idea. Can you help me get Miles up to the treehouse?"

Miles was hard to wake up - they each slung an arm over their shoulders and dragged him to the ladder, his feet bumping along limply behind them. He started to come to, and groggily climbed the ladder.

Willis' arms and legs were sore as he followed Miles up and hiked himself through the opening. Willis sat down, his back against the wall, his legs crooked in front of him.

Miles woke up a bit, his head bobbing up, startled, and looked around. His eyes widened in alarm when he saw Willis.

"You again!"

"We've been here before - do you remember?"

said Willis. "Look, here's your name." He pointed to the scratched-in word with triangular letters, "MILES."

"Miles," Miles read, his fingers tracing the letters. "I - I don't know."

"You still don't remember us? Either of us?"

Willis turned and looked at Sala. She looked back, then down in disappointment. A wave of exhaustion washed over him.

Willis' body ached. What was he doing here?

He closed his eyes to think, rummaging through memories, and stopped at a memory of sitting right where they were. The sun was warm, the air was sweet and the treehouse rocked gently and creaked as a breeze soughed in the trees.

He, Willis, was inside, leaning against one of the walls. Through his thin T-shirt he could feel the gap between the rough boards with his back. There, sitting at the door at the side of the treehouse, was Miles. He was looking out over the field, dangling his legs and kicking his feet. He was smiling and chattering, though Willis couldn't make out what he was saying.

Then Willis had a rush of memories, as if someone had dumped out a shelf full of books. He remembered playing games with Miles under towering elms in the summer twilight, the darkening sky a deep crystal blue, the lawn a blue-black-green beneath it. The two of them crammed into a snow tunnel, expanding a subterranean chamber lying on their backs and kicking wildly with their boots. Standing in a deep puddle in the back yard in springtime, his foot sinking deeper and deeper into soft mud as the icy cold waters got closer and closer to the top of his boot, shouting at Miles to get help. The time Miles brought back a real live snake from a trip to the country with his uncle.

Willis opened his eyes. He was back in the grey treehouse, a cold wind whistling through the gaps. His fingers were nearly numb, and he stuffed them into the pockets of his sweatshirt. His hand brushed against something hard and round, with a waxy surface, and closed on it. He pulled it out.

It was a granny smith apple. Willis held it up to his nose, and tried to catch its scent. His nose had cleared a little, and he could catch a tiny whiff of sour aroma.

"Here," Willis said holding out the apple to Miles. "Take a bite."

Miles reached out and nervously took the apple, eyeing it closely.

"Go on. Take a bite," said Willis.

Miles shrugged. He bit into it, with a great crunch chewed and swallowed. A little trickle of apple juice ran from the corner of his mouth.

A light went on in his eyes. He looked back and forth between Willis and Sala, and suddenly burst into tears. His body was shaking, and he was very quiet, but the tears were streaming down his face. He had a great intake of breath, a gasping sob, and started laughing - also silently, tears still streaming down his face, all of his straight white teeth in a smile he couldn't break.

He paused, gasped, looked back and forth

between them and started laughing again. He was shaking his head and giggling, wagging a limp finger in Willis' direction.

Finally he calmed down enough, wiping his eyes.

"I remember. I remember you Willis. I remember the time you were stuck in a puddle, sinking in the mud, and I watched as your boot got deeper and deeper. And I remember you, Sala. I remember playing hide and seek under the porch."

"And I remember," he took a deep shuddering breath, and his voice started to crack, "I remember my mom." He sobbed again, then wiped his nose with his arm, smiled and took a deep breath.

"Can I go home now?"

Willis looked at Sala, who nodded.

"Here, shuffle over in front of the door," said Willis.

Miles scooted over.

"I'll see you on the other side," said Willis, and lunged forward, pushing Miles out. Miles tumbled out and back toward the ground, arms windmilling, then vanished, leaving a circular puff of dust and twitching grass.

"We're done," said Sala. "He'll be home soon, knocking at his mother's door."

"What about you?" asked Willis.

"What about me?"

"How do we wake you up? You're not one of those weird things from three dreams deep. You don't belong here. You must have parents somewhere too."

"I just - don't know," she said, looking miserable, when just a moment before she seemed so happy and relieved. Her eyes were filling with tears.

"I'm sorry," said Willis. "I didn't mean to make you sad. But I don't want you to be lonely again."

He edged closer to her and brushed a tear away from her cheek. She was very pretty, he thought, and her mouth was trembling slightly as she kept from crying.

He pushed her hair back and leaned in to kiss her, with one hand on her side.

At first she seemed barely there, like she was a shell made of paper, her lips like flower petals, cool but as substantial as a puff of air. Then he could feel her lips press back, soft and warm. And her body under his hand too was surprisingly warm and solid and real. He could feel her ribs under his fingers.

They embraced, awkwardly since both were kneeling, and she wrapped her arm around his neck. He could feel her hot breath at his ear, whispering a nearly inaudible, "I remember."

He glanced at her face. She was smiling through tears. They each sat back. Willis could feel his face burning red. It was the first time he had kissed anyone.

"It's time to wake up," she said, and pushed him out of the treehouse.

CHAPTER 10
AFTER

WILLIS WOKE to find his father shaking him awake.

"Willis - for God's sake, wake up!"

He was in his room. A lightning flash lit up his father's face - looking weird without his glasses, his hair matted and crazed. There was a drum-roll of hard rain against the windowpanes followed by a rumbling crash of thunder.

"Are you all right? You were screaming bloody murder."

Willis yanked his arm out of his father's hands. He couldn't shake the feeling of that mouth on his arm, completely separate from his father's grip.

He was groggy.

"Willis - are you alright?" His dad flicked on the bedside lamp. Willis winced, then brought his eyes to focus on his father's face in the yellow light of the lamp. He looked so worried.

"You've been asleep around the clock. You must have come down with something."

Willis lifted his head and tried to say something, but his tongue seemed thick, his face almost frozen.

"S'alright, dad. I - s'just - a dream," he slumped back to his pillow.

His dad put his hand on Willis' forehead.

"You're sweating," he said. "But I can't tell if you've got a fever. Let me get your mother. Honey!" his dad called into the hallway. "Can you come check Willis' temperature?

"Just wanna sleep," said Willis, trying to curl

up in his blankets.

His mother appeared from around the corner.

"What's happening - is he alright? Oh! Did you knock your face on something? Your nose is bleeding."

Willis touched his hand to his lip and found it sticky.

"Let me at least clean you up," his mom said, disappearing from the room.

"No - no," Willis mumbled, then dozed for what seemed like seconds, when a rough washcloth soaked in hot water was being thrust under his nose, scrubbing away at his face.

"There. Now you're tidy," his mother placed a cool dry hand on his damp forehead. "You can go back to sleep."

"I'm OK," he mumbled.

•

Willis came down late for breakfast to the smoky smell of burning butter in a hot pan, which meant pancakes. He found his dad at the stove.

"Hi Willis. Are you feeling all right?"

"Yeah," said Willis, clearing his throat and

scratching his head. "I'm hungry."

"Well, that's a sign you're on the mend."

The kitchen door slammed. It was his mom, bringing a blast of cool air with her, and peeling off a long woolen scarf, a brown grocery bag in the crook of her arm.

"I've got the most amazing story for you. You will never believe what just happened to Meg. After all these years her son, Miles, shows up on her front step out of nowhere? She's a changed woman. I've never heard her so happy. They were just hugging and crying, she looks twenty years younger! Well, let's be honest, ten."

"That's incredible," said his dad. "Just incredible. Where was he? When he went missing I never thought he would ever be found again."

"No explanation. I don't think Meg cares. She's too busy planning renovations and whatnot. Willis, she wants you to go over to play with him!"

Willis grunted.

"Do we have any lemon and sugar for the pancakes?" he asked.

His parents stared.

"Willis," said his mom, "This is an amazing story. You don't seem impressed in the least. Miles vanished without a trace years ago and he's suddenly back? It's a miracle!"

"If you say so," said Willis.

His parents continued to stare back at him.

"I am impressed!" he said. "I'm just really hungry! Dad, I think you're burning the pancakes."

With a loud "Darnit!" his dad turned back to the stove, lifting edges and inspecting for char, then stage-whistling his relief when he found them unburnt.

"I want you to take a care package over there later on," said his mom, as his dad slid a plateful of food in front of him.

"Sure," said Willis.

"Oh, before I forget," his dad said. "There's a phone message for you. Sala called. Said for you to call her at home."

He slid a scrap of paper across the table with

a name and number scrawled on it. Willis stared at it, a fork loaded with pancake suspended in the air.

Call Sala at home.

He looked up to find his parents looking at him with strange grins on their faces. Did they know?

"What?" he asked them.

His dad turned to his mom. "We can't give him too much of a hard time about getting calls from girls."

Willis looked at his left forearm, reached over with his right hand, grabbed a tuck of skin and pinched it hard, hurting himself.

"Ow!" he said, rubbing the spot.

"What are you doing?" his mother asked.

"Just making sure I'm not dreaming," he said, and smiled to himself.

THE END

ABOUT THE AUTHOR

D.F. (Dougald) Lamont is a writer, designer, musician and filmmaker. He lives in Winnipeg, Canada with his wife and children. He's been writing professionally for 20 years.

Three Dreams Deep is his second book. His first book, "The Jinx" is much acclaimed, and is available in paperback and as an e-book.

You can find updates on his writing at:

http://DFLamont.tumblr.com

and facebook.com/TheJinxbyDFLamont